**Dear Reader,**

Ever since I was a little girl, I've dreamed of living in a fairy-tale castle. One with the whole works, including stone turrets, a drawbridge and complete with its very own prince, of course!

Living in the gorgeous city of Melbourne, castles are a little thin on the ground, so I had to create my own. I'm so lucky!

When Dante Andretti, Prince of Calida, arrives in Melbourne, hotelier Natasha Telford is prepared to meet and greet yet another VIP. However, Dante isn't your average prince, and Natasha soon finds herself envisioning that very same dream I had of living in a castle. Only she gets to do it for real!

I hope you enjoy reading the romantic tale of my sexy prince and how he meets his match!

Best wishes,

*Nicola*

D0833044

## The guy looked like a walking advertisement for Bad Boys Inc.

Tall, over six feet, with broad shoulders hugged in soft gray cotton, long lean legs encased in faded denim, black wavy hair mussed by a helmet and a gusty southerly Melbourne wind, and a bone structure that could've been chiseled by one of the Italian masters.

"I need this sorted now, and you're just the woman I want."

His low, gravelly voice sent an unexpected shiver down her spine, and her smile faltered as he fixed her with a penetrating stare.

Those eyes…that color…no way! It couldn't be.

His voice dropped lower as he leaned across the desk, barely inches from her face, enveloping her in a heady scent that reminded her of hot cross buns: warm and sweet and cinnamon. Yum.

"I think you've been expecting me? I'm Dante Andretti."

Natasha gripped the desk to steady her wobbly legs.

This couldn't be happening.

No way could this guy be the prince.

# NICOLA MARSH

*Princess Australia*

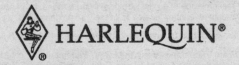

TORONTO • NEW YORK • LONDON
AMSTERDAM • PARIS • SYDNEY • HAMBURG
STOCKHOLM • ATHENS • TOKYO • MILAN • MADRID
PRAGUE • WARSAW • BUDAPEST • AUCKLAND

If you purchased this book without a cover you should be aware that this book is stolen property. It was reported as "unsold and destroyed" to the publisher, and neither the author nor the publisher has received any payment for this "stripped book."

ISBN-13: 978-0-373-18306-7
ISBN-10:  0-373-18306-2

PRINCESS AUSTRALIA

First North American Publication 2007.

Copyright © 2007 by Nicola Marsh.

All rights reserved. Except for use in any review, the reproduction or utilization of this work in whole or in part in any form by any electronic, mechanical or other means, now known or hereafter invented, including xerography, photocopying and recording, or in any information storage or retrieval system, is forbidden without the written permission of the publisher, Harlequin Enterprises Limited, 225 Duncan Mill Road, Don Mills, Ontario, Canada M3B 3K9.

This is a work of fiction. Names, characters, places and incidents are either the product of the author's imagination or are used fictitiously, and any resemblance to actual persons, living or dead, business establishments, events or locales is entirely coincidental.

This edition published by arrangement with Harlequin Books S.A.

® and TM are trademarks of the publisher. Trademarks indicated with ® are registered in the United States Patent and Trademark Office, the Canadian Trade Marks Office and in other countries.

www.eHarlequin.com

Printed in U.S.A.

**Nicola Marsh** has always had a passion for writing and reading. As a youngster, she devoured books when she should have been sleeping, and later kept a diary, which could be an epic in itself! These days, when she's not enjoying life with her husband and son in her home city of Melbourne, she's at her computer doing her dream job creating the romances she loves. Visit Nicola's Web site at www.nicolamarsh.com for the latest news of her books.

For the real princesses in my life.

Thanks for your warmth, your friendship
and the many laughs we share.

# CHAPTER ONE

'I WANT a crate of soda, a monster bowl of hot chips and a triple layered choc-fudge banana-split sundae. Got that? And make it snappy!'

Natasha Telford glared at the back of Australia's youngest pop star as he strutted towards the lift after snapping his order at her. She surreptitiously squeezed a stress ball under the concierge's desk while wishing she could rip a few more slashes into the upstart's trendy torn T-shirt.

How old Harvey did this job on a daily basis she'd never know.

As a kid growing up in Telford Towers, she'd thought the concierge had the most glamorous job in the world. Until this week, when she'd had to fill in while Harvey had his hip replacement. Giving polite tourists directions to Melbourne's famous sites she could handle. It was the sulky, rude, demanding famous—especially young punks barely out of school—she could politely strangle.

Speaking of famous, the Prince of Calida was due any second, and she cast a quick, assessing look around the lobby, ensuring everything was in place. The demanding little snot of a pop star could wait for his sundae. She had a bigger guy to impress, namely Dante Andretti, soon to be crowned monarch of a tiny principality off Italy's west coast, if the info she'd gleaned off the Net was accurate.

The lobby looked perfect, from its polished marble floor to gleaming brass-trimmed check-in desk, its plush chocolate-brown sofas and muted antique lamps with the stunning floral bouquets ordered on a daily basis arranged strategically throughout.

Natasha smiled, infused with the same pride she experienced every day she entered the Towers. She loved this place. Every last square inch of it. And she'd do anything to make sure it stayed in the family. Anything.

'So when's His Uptightness due?'

Natasha's smile broadened as she whirled around and came face to face with Ella Worchester, her best friend.

'Don't call him that. He's probably a really nice guy,' she said, rearranging a pile of maps, a box of theatre tickets and a credenza of tourist flyers for the umpteenth time. Her nerves were working overtime, and if the prince didn't arrive soon she'd go into serious meltdown.

Ella rolled her eyes and stuck her ink-stained hands in the pockets of her low-slung denim hipsters. 'Yeah, I bet he's a real prince.'

Natasha ignored Ella's cynicism as she usually did. Right now, a prince was exactly what she needed—or, more accurately, what the Towers needed.

'Do you know much about him?'

Not enough. And that was what had her worried.

Usually, she knew everything about the VIPs staying at the hotel. It was her job. In this case, even more vital than usual. Telford Towers needed the prince's presence, like, yesterday.

Natasha shrugged. 'Only what I've gleaned off the Net, which isn't much. There was a whole heap of geographical stuff about Calida, a tiny bit about the royal family and that's about it.'

'Is he cute?' Ella stuck out a slender hip in a provocative pose, and Natasha laughed.

'Couldn't tell much from the pic on the website. Too small.'

'You wouldn't be holding out on me by any

chance?' Ella's teasing tone elicited more laughter and Natasha held up her hands in surrender.

'Give me a break. From what I could see, the guy was trussed up like a turkey in some fancy-schmancy uniform, had his hair slicked back in army fashion and looked like he couldn't crack a smile if his life depended on it. There, satisfied?'

Though there was one thing that had stood out in the prince's picture.

His eyes.

Beautiful, clear blue eyes that had leapt off her computer screen and imprinted on her brain.

She'd always had a thing for guys' eyes, believing in the whole 'windows to the soul' thing. Pity she hadn't read the real motivation behind Clay's eyes. It would've saved her a lot of heartache, and would've avoided putting her family in the invidious position of losing the one thing that meant everything, courtesy of her greedy ex.

'Well, don't let him boss you around, okay? You're only filling in for Harvey; doesn't mean you have to take anything from anyone, prince or not.'

Natasha squeezed Ella's hand. 'The prince is important for business, and I'll treat him like I treat the rest of the customers. With respect, care and—'

'Yeah, yeah. Save the spiel for someone who hasn't heard it a million times before.' Ella held up her hand, though her fond grin underlined the lack of malice in her words. 'Now, if you don't mind, I have a gardening column to write and a few more botanical drawings to do before lunch.'

'Coffee at Trevi's, usual time?' By then, she'd definitely need a caffeine hit.

'Sounds great. See you at five.'

Ella gave her a cheeky wave and sauntered away, a slim, tall figure in head-to-toe denim with her short, shaggy auburn bob swinging in sync with her steps.

Her best friend was stunning, enjoyed life and had energy to burn, while Natasha felt like a worn facecloth wrung dry. Stress did that to a person, the type of stress that dogged her every waking moment, and unfortunately most of her sleeping ones too. Little wonder she looked so pale next to her vibrant friend.

Glancing at her gold and silver link watch—the one her dad had given her for her twenty-first, years before money had become a problem for them—she wondered why the prince was late. Most of the VIPs she usually dealt with had their itineraries scheduled to the last second and she assumed royalty would be more pedantic than most.

Especially a prince who looked like he couldn't crack a smile, if that tiny pic on the Net had been any indication.

At that moment, a gleaming black Harley roared to a stop outside the front door, and Natasha nibbled nervously on her bottom lip, hoping Alan the doorman would get the noisy thing valet-parked as soon as possible. First impressions counted, and she desperately needed to make this one count with the prince.

After another nervous glance at her watch, and more subtle rearranging of the tourist brochures stacked on the concierge desk, she glanced up in time to see the Harley's rider stride through the glass doors.

And her mouth went dry.

The guy looked like a walking advertisement for Bad Boys Inc: tall, over six feet, with broad shoulders hugged in soft grey cotton, long lean legs encased in faded denim, black wavy hair mussed by a helmet and a gusty southerly Melbourne wind, and a bone structure that could've been chiselled by one of the Italian masters.

Natasha took a deep breath, closed her eyes and tried to refocus. What on earth was she doing? So the guy looked like every woman's fantasy come to life—since when did she have time to ogle guys, let alone lose her concentration on the job?

Especially at a time like this!

Mentally slapping herself for letting her long-dormant hormones get the better of her in that one, glorious moment when he strode into the foyer, she exhaled and opened her eyes, ready to march out onto the street and haul the prince into her hotel the minute his limo pulled up.

Being antsy was getting the better of her and making her think all sorts of crazy things, like how much she'd like to walk up to the sexy bad boy and ask in her best, sultriest voice, 'Can I help you?'

He saved her the trouble.

'I need your help.'

Natasha quickly smoothed her cuff over her watch—she really had to stop glancing at it every five seconds—and fixed her professional welcoming smile in place. However, her smile froze when she looked up and locked gazes with the bad boy.

Clear blue eyes.

Almost aquamarine, the mesmerising colour of the Great Barrier Reef on a sunny day.

A colour imprinted in her memory banks, considering it was the only stand-out feature she could remember from the prince's fuzzy picture.

'Miss Telford, is it?'

The bad boy glanced at her name tag before

returning his gaze to her face. A face flushed with heat at the realisation that she really must be losing the plot if she thought for one second that this scruffy, wind-tossed guy could be the Prince of Calida.

She really needed a day off to unwind. Badly.

'Yes, that's right. What can I do for you?'

*Apart from bustle you out of here and get ready for the most important meeting of my life.*

'Plenty, hopefully.'

He rested his forearms on the desk, and she tried not to stare at the way his biceps bunched at the simple action.

Oh boy, maybe she needed to change her whole non-dating policy. It had been eighteen months since the Clayton disaster, and she hadn't been out with a guy since, preferring to concentrate on fixing the mess Clay had lumbered her family with.

Resisting the urge to take a peek over his shoulder towards the door in case the prince snuck in without her seeing, she said, 'Do you have a reservation, sir? If not, perhaps I can arrange it with someone at Check-in and we can discuss your needs later?'

'No, I need this sorted now, and you're just the woman I want.'

His low, gravelly voice sent an unexpected

shiver down her spine, and her smile faltered as he fixed her with a penetrating stare.

Those eyes…that colour…no way!

It couldn't be.

His voice dropped lower as he leaned across the desk barely inches from her face, enveloping her in a heady scent that reminded her of hot cross buns: warm and sweet and cinnamon. *Yum.*

'I think you've been expecting me. I'm Dante Andretti.'

Natasha gripped the desk to steady her wobbly legs.

This couldn't be happening.

No way could this guy be the prince.

'The Prince of Calida,' he added as an afterthought, the corners of his mouth lifting in a small, sexy smile which did strange things to Natasha's insides, things she'd never felt before, things she had no right to experience now.

He was the prince.

This…this…*rebel* was the man she'd pinned all her hopes on for saving her father's business?

Lord help her.

'Is there a problem, Miss Telford?'

Swallowing her first response of 'you bet your sweet butt there is', she said, 'Not at all, Your Highness.'

'Ssh!' He shook his head vigorously and put an index finger to his lips, like some second-rate spy. 'Someone might hear you.'

'And that might be a problem because…?' Her voice held a slight tinge of hysteria, and she took a few steadying breaths.

This was crazy. It had to be one of those stupid *Candid Camera* stunts where her dad and Ella would leap out at any moment and say 'Gotcha!'

She'd expected the prince to arrive in a stretch limo; this guy had revved in on a motorbike.

She'd expected the prince to have an entourage of bodyguards; this guy was solo.

She'd expected a stiff upper lip, hair-slicked-back pompous ass, and this guy was laid back, ruffled and very, very sexy.

Way too sexy.

'In case you hadn't noticed, I'm not advertising my identity and I'd like to keep it that way.'

Natasha sighed, wishing for one ounce of the kind of saint-like patience that Ella demonstrated when she sat for hours in front of a plant to sketch it. 'I'm not following this. You're booked in under your real name but you don't want anyone to know you're here?'

He snapped his fingers under her nose, his smile broadening. 'Exactly.'

No, no, no!

Natasha wanted to stamp her feet like one of her rock-star guests having a tantrum.

This wouldn't do. She needed to broadcast the prince's presence in her hotel to the world, and he wanted to keep it a secret? Was the guy out of his mind?

'Is there a security problem? Something I should know about?' *Like why you've turned up here looking like a jeans model and spouting a whole lot of nonsense?*

'No problem. But I would like a chance to talk further. Like I said, I need your help while I'm here. Let me check in, and perhaps we can meet when you've finished your shift, yes?'

'No!'

Natasha lowered her voice, deriving some satisfaction from the surprised glint in those too-blue eyes. Good. Let him see how it felt to be on the receiving end of a few surprises for once. She'd had her quota for the day.

'No?'

Schooling her face into what she hoped was a professional mask, she said, 'What I meant was I'm busy here for the next few hours. It will be a while before I finish up.'

'No matter.' He waved his hand as if her answer meant little, and she suddenly realised that though this guy didn't look like a prince he had the commanding mannerisms down pat. 'I will wait. I'm booked in as Dan Anders.'

Her mouth twitched, the first time she'd felt like smiling since this crazy, prince-imperson-ating-a-bad-boy had strode into her hotel.

'Nice pseudonym.'

He shrugged, and she stared at those muscles again, the way they bunched and shifted beneath the cotton T-shirt, and she wondered if they felt as firm as they looked.

'Dante Andretti, Dan Anders. I chose some-thing similar not to confuse myself.'

His self-deprecating grin displayed a row of even white teeth, made more startling by his sensational tan.

She knew pictures often didn't do their subjects justice. In the prince's case, he should have the royal photographer shot.

The guy was gorgeous, impressively so. And for a girl who had sworn off guys after Clay that was saying something.

So she wasn't blind. She could look, couldn't she? Like window shopping; you didn't have to touch—oops, she meant buy—the merchandise!

'Why don't we meet in the Lobby Bar for a coffee around four-thirty? I have plans at five.'

There was no way she'd be popping into this

guy's room for a rendezvous, prince or not. She had a reputation to uphold in this place, not to mention the fact he unnerved her with that steady, blue-eyed stare.

He shrugged. 'Fine. I'm not surprised a beautiful woman like you would have plans.'

Okay, so she could add charm to his list of impressive attributes.

'Right,' she said, suddenly flustered when he didn't look away, her hands fiddling with the stress ball behind the desk. 'We'll talk about this more then, but let me tell you, I'm not happy about this situation. I don't like lies, I don't like subterfuge, and having you stay at our hotel is important for business.'

On and on she babbled, hating the way his mouth curved deliciously at the corners, the way his eyes glinted with amusement, and the way she kept noticing inconsequential details like that.

She was making a fool of herself, sounding like an uptight schoolmarm scolding a recalcitrant kid. She always did that when she was nervous, getting all defensive and huffy. Ella teased her about it. Sadly, she spent too much time these days on the defensive.

'We'll talk about this business later, then, Miss Telford.'

'Call me Natasha,' she said, a blush heating

her cheeks for some inexplicable reason. Gee, it wasn't like she was telling him to call her for a date or anything!

'Dante.'

His polite nod reaffirmed what she'd thought earlier: you could take the bad boy out of the prince but you couldn't take the prince out of the bad boy.

'See you at four-thirty.'

She managed a tight smile, the type of smile that made her teeth ache with the effort. This cloak and dagger business with Dante reeked of trouble.

Big trouble.

And she'd had enough of that lately to last a lifetime.

# CHAPTER TWO

DANTE cast subtle glances Natasha's way while an efficient young woman checked him in.

She intrigued him.

He was used to subservience, deference and awe when people learned his identity, but the stunning brunette hadn't batted an eyelid. In fact, she'd grown more prickly, tension radiating off her in palpable waves.

She didn't like him.

That much was obvious, and he wanted to know why. Maybe she had a hang-up about wealth? Or maybe his title?

No matter. The minute he'd set foot in the hotel, he'd known he would need the concierge onside if he was to perpetrate his plan. The fact the concierge was a gorgeous woman with caramel eyes, long legs and a fabulous body behind that frumpy dark green uniform just made his task all the easier.

Not that he could rely on charming the woman to his way of thinking. If anything, she'd give him a hard time, he just knew it. Her little holier-than-thou speech had been a dead giveaway that Miss Natasha Telford wouldn't stand for any hanky-panky. Not that he had any in mind. Not really…

'Here's your welcome pack, Mr Anders. The card for your room is inside. Enjoy your stay at Telford Towers.'

He smiled his thanks at the young woman behind the check-in desk, grabbed his key and headed for the lifts.

Of course, it wasn't his fault he had to pass directly in front of the concierge's desk again, and it definitely wasn't his fault that the sexy concierge chose that exact moment to look up.

He gave her his best smile, the one his mother said could rule Calida alone, and a half salute, enjoying the faint blush staining her cheeks.

So, she wasn't immune to a little charm after all?

He'd have to remember that.

His plan to remain anonymous on the first leg of his trip might depend on it.

Natasha rifled through her wardrobe, flicking past formal dresses, sundresses, skirts and casual trousers before coming to rest on her favourite pair of jeans. At times like this, being super-organised—or obsessively tidy, as Ella liked to tease—was a definite plus. She'd dithered long enough.

Sliding the worn denim off the hanger, she wriggled into them, noting with irony the only good thing Clay had left her with was a slimmer figure. Stressing out over what he'd cost her and her family had shed pounds by the bucketful, and she'd never been so thin.

After slipping a fitted pink singlet top over her head, pulling her hair back in a low ponytail, fixing silver hoops in her ears and sliding her feet into black wedges, she stood back and stared in the floor-length mirror behind the door.

Her favourite outfit, the type of outfit that made her feel good, that gave her confidence.

Then why did she want to rip it off and pull a serious black dress over her head?

*You're a fraud, that's why.*

She poked her tongue out at her reflection, hating when her subconscious was right. No matter how casual she tried to dress, or how confident her clothes were supposed to make her feel, she was a mess.

Dealing with Dante Andretti would've been

hard enough without the runaway prince playing some weird rebel game where he wanted to hide his identity. The same identity she needed to shout from the rooftops to boost the hotel's profile and, ultimately, save it.

'Damn it,' she muttered, dashing a slick of gloss across her lips and waving a mascara wand over her lashes, knowing it would take a heck of a lot more than a bit of make-up to give her a much needed boost.

She needed the prince's help.

Apparently, he needed hers.

Then why the awful, sinking feeling their needs were poles apart? Or, worse, she'd be coerced into putting his first...and all because of a charming smile and a pair of blue eyes that had haunted her memory since the first time she'd seen them in grainy print on a computer screen.

Why couldn't he be a boring, fuddy-duddy prince hell-bent on performing normal royal duties—like getting his face on every media outlet?

Why was he masquerading as some sexy bad boy? Okay, so he couldn't help the sexy part but, honestly, wasn't he taking the whole rebel image a tad far? How did a guy like that own a pair of worn jeans anyway? Wouldn't he wear perfectly pleated formal trousers all the time?

And why did he specifically need *her* help to perpetrate whatever game he was playing?

Determined to get answers to the questions swirling in her mind, Natasha picked up her keys and purse and headed for a rendezvous with a prince.

Dante glanced around the cosy bar, surprised by the homey feel. He'd travelled the world, stayed in the best hotels and sampled the finest luxuries money could buy, yet something about this place tugged at him.

The rich, mahogany coffee-tables and bar covering an entire back wall, the deep comfy armchairs in burgundy, the muted light from brass lamps and the scattering of antiques were nothing out of the ordinary. Yet together they created an ambience which beckoned like the privacy of his own room at the palace at the end of a long day.

Suddenly it hit him—the privacy aspect of the room, the same comforting feeling he'd expect from a private lounge, not some hotel lobby bar. That was it. This room beckoned like his sitting room back home.

Someone had gone to a lot of trouble to create this effect, to offer travellers a home away from home. Someone with taste, good business sense and a keen sense of what it felt like to belong.

At that moment, Natasha walked into the room, and his desire to admire the decor went up in smoke.

He smiled and waved her over, mesmerised by the sway of her slim hips in poured-on denim, the way the lamplight highlighted the toffee tints in her hair, and how her overall outfit combined sassy casual with an innate elegance. Though he guessed that had more to do with the woman inside the clothes than the garments themselves.

Natasha Telford, quite simply, took his breath away.

Now he only hoped she had an open mind to go along with his plan.

'Glad you could make it,' he said, rising to his feet and pulling out a chair.

'No problems.' She inclined her head in thanks and sat down, gesturing to a waiter behind the bar. 'What would you like?'

'Espresso, please.' *And a healthy dollop of your co-operation.*

'Make that two,' she said, smiling at the waiter in a way that made Dante's pulse roar.

Why couldn't she give him one of those smiles? Was the young guy a flame?

He studied her carefully, watching for a flushing of cheeks, a coy expression, a change in body language, but he came up blank. In fact, while he'd been making a few irrational leaps of thought it looked like she'd been studying him just as intently. By the slight frown marring her smooth forehead, he'd come up lacking.

'So what did you want to discuss?'

She sat ramrod-straight, her hands clasped firmly in her lap, a determined look on her face, and Dante had a sneaking suspicion his plan was about to hit a major snag in the form of one beautiful wet blanket.

'I need your help.'

'So you said earlier.'

Her caustic tone didn't inspire much confidence and he ploughed on, choosing his words carefully.

'My visit to your country is multi-faceted. Official duties, fostering foreign relations and a family visit. Everyone knows the prince will be staying at your hotel and for how long. What they don't know is that I've arrived on schedule, assumed a different identity and will have my secretary ring to say I've been delayed by a week. So during that week I wish to remain anonymous.'

'Why didn't you let me know your need for anonymity when you booked?'

Good question; he just couldn't give her an honest answer. How could he explain to a woman he barely knew that the spur of the moment decision had as much to do with a desperate need to escape as his desire to spend time with a nephew he'd hardly seen?

'My extra week here is impromptu and I need some time out from my duties.'

She raised an eyebrow, a delicate gesture that made him smile. Somehow, he knew there was nothing delicate about Natasha Telford. She came across as a vision of feminine loveliness...with a backbone of steel beneath.

'I see.'

By the tiny frown creasing her brow, he seriously doubted that.

'For family reasons?'

'Uh-huh.'

Natasha sat back in the armchair and fixed the prince with a suspicious glare, wondering if he thought she were completely stupid.

Guys like him didn't flit around countries trying to hide their identity for 'family reasons'. They did the whole cloak and dagger thing for floozies, mistresses or whatever the name was for their hidden love interests.

The prince must have a secret lover, someone he didn't want the press to get wind of, and that had to be the real reason behind this elaborate farce.

So what? It wasn't any of her business. As long as he came out of the closet—so to speak—at the end of the week, she'd still get the much-needed publicity boost for the Towers. And, after playing along with His Sneaky Highness, she had every intention of milking his royal presence for every cent he was worth.

'You don't look too impressed.'

Silently cursing her expressive face, Natasha said, 'What you do in the next week is no concern of mine.'

'That's where you're wrong.'

The arrival of their espressos put paid to the questions raging through her brain, and she waited till they were alone again to continue.

'I don't follow.'

'You are the only person who knows my real identity and I want it to stay that way. It is imperative. Do I make myself clear?'

She stared at him in open-mouthed shock. Who did he think he was, talking down to her like that?

Then again, he was a prince, and obviously used to ordering people around. Not to mention the guy who would get her family's business out of crisis.

She'd bite her tongue. For now.

'Perfectly clear,' she said, taking a sip of her coffee, enjoying the caffeine rush and trying not to notice the way his long, tanned fingers wrapped around the tall glass mug with ease, as if they were made to hold things…caress things…

'Good.'

He stared at her over the rim of his mug, those blue eyes capturing her attention and making it impossible to look away no matter how much she wanted to.

'How long have you been a concierge?'

His question came out of left field though she should have been grateful. With his probing stare, she'd half expected something more personal.

'Less than a week.'

He lowered his mug, surprise etched across his handsome face. 'By your surname, I assumed you were part of the Telford family and in the job for a long time. Maybe I've en-trusted my secret to the wrong person?'

'Relax,' she said, enjoying her first genuine smile of their meeting.

No matter how laid back His Highness seemed, this whole secrecy thing was getting to him. She could see it in his suddenly tense shoulders, his rigid neck, his clenched fingers. His floozy must be some woman for him to go to these lengths to protect her identity.

'My father runs Telford Towers and I've worked here since I could walk. Our concierge is away for the next twelve weeks on sick leave, so I'm filling in for seven days till his temporary replacement starts next week. Does that allay your fears?'

He nodded and visibly relaxed, placing his mug on the table between them and leaning back in his chair. 'So, what do you usually do here?'

'Everything.'

From ensuring things ran smoothly, to mediating staff disputes, to pampering VIPs, she did it all. It was what she loved about this place, had always loved about it. Being a part of Telford Towers came as naturally to her as breathing and she couldn't let it slip away.

Especially when this entire mess with Clay was her fault.

'Such as?'

She should've been flattered by Dante's interest, but she wasn't a fool. Now that he had her here, he wanted to know every last thing about the only person who knew his little secret. He probably still didn't trust her.

'I'm my father's right-hand woman. After I graduated with an MBA, I joined him in the everyday running of the Towers. Whatever needs to be done, I do it.'

His eyes widened, the admiration in the steady blue gaze warming her from the inside out. 'Is it only the two of you?'

'Uh-huh.'

And the painful fact ripped through her, re-opening old wounds. Would her mum have survived the heart attack without the added stress Clay had brought upon them? Would Natasha have to spend the rest of her life har-bouring the unspeakable guilt that she had con-tributed to her mum's death as well as potentially ruining the family?

'You should be proud. Your father and you have done a marvellous job. This hotel is won-derful. This is wonderful.'

He threw his arms wide in a dramatic gesture characteristic of his Italian heritage, and she managed a tiny smile when in fact she felt like bolting to the sanctity of her room and bawling her eyes out. Memories of her mum always made her feel like crying.

'Did you hire a designer to create this room?'

Natasha shook her head, a burst of pride

making her sit up straighter, and she quelled the urge to sniffle. 'I did it.'

'Really?'

If his eyebrows shot any higher, they would've reached the elaborate cornices lining the patterned ceiling.

'That's right. I wanted to create a home away from home for weary travellers. It's the type of room I'd like to spend time in if I was stuck in a hotel miles away from everything familiar.'

Her voice rose as she spoke, filled with excitement, and she marvelled at the sudden change. It had been a long time since she'd felt anything bar intense, draining responsibility. She'd made a major mess of things and she had to clean it up.

Where every day used to bring joy and a thrill as she flitted from task to task, the last year had brought nothing but guilt, recrimination and a weary determination to do a job she used to love wholeheartedly.

But that was all about to change. Starting with the prince-playing-hooky sitting in front of her, if he agreed to help.

'You've captured the exact feeling I had when I first sat down,' he said, glancing around the room with a sparkle in his eyes before his gaze came to rest on her. 'You're a very talented woman.'

'Thank you.'

She blushed, an annoying surge of heat that probably made her look like a sideshow clown. Somehow, his simple compliment meant more to her than all the accolades she'd received in the hotel business.

She really was in a soppy mood. Time to escape before she did something silly like beg him to head up the Towers' next ad campaign or, better yet, grovel in the hope he would book out the Presidential Suite for the next decade. Both would be financial boons and either option would get them out of trouble.

Making an obvious show of glancing at her watch, she said, 'If our meeting here is over, I really must go.'

The cheeky glint in his eyes faded. 'Ah, yes, your secret assignation.'

*That's your game, bucko, not mine.*

Thankfully, she bit back that retort. 'Nothing too secret about meeting my best friend for our daily catch-up at our favourite trattoria.'

She could've sworn she saw relief in his eyes before his super-sexy smile drew her attention. 'You meet your friend every day?'

She nodded, knowing she would never have survived the last few years without brash, exuberant Ella, the sweetest, most loyal friend a girl could ever wish for. The two of them had met through Telford Towers when Ella had moved into one of the apartments five years ago.

The dastardly duo, her mum had called them.

Natasha preferred 'dynamic duo' because that's how great Ella made her feel. Her best friend was reliable and loads of fun. And it seemed like so long since she'd had any.

'Yeah, keeps us sane. Nothing better than unwinding over a latte at the end of a hard day.'

'You are lucky.'

He shrugged, a simple, eloquent gesture that spoke volumes when combined with the wistful tone in his voice.

At that precise moment, Natasha could've sworn the prince sounded lonely. Very lonely.

'I know. Now, I'm sorry, but I really must dash.'

She stood quickly, eager to put distance between them before she leaned over and gave him a comforting hug. He looked like he needed one.

Though maybe that had more to do with her crazy hormones coming to life after a few glimpses of his muscled chest beneath cotton?

Either way, she wasn't sticking around.

'Thank you for agreeing to meet with me.

And for agreeing to assist with that other matter.' He stood and gave a strange, little formal bow which made her want to giggle, considering his bad-boy outfit.

Guys with day-old stubble, unruly hair and faded denim didn't bow. They rode motorbikes and broke hearts maybe, but bowing? *Uh-uh*.

'If you need anything, don't hesitate to contact me,' she said out of habit as she grabbed her purse and stood.

Not that His Sneaky Highness would need anything more of her. She bet he had his whole week planned out, starting with a rendezvous with the royal floozy.

'How do you propose I do that?'

She halted, surprised by the hint of urgency in his voice. 'Uh…through Reception.'

He sent her a sceptical look as if knowing she was giving him the brush-off.

Okay, so it wouldn't be too smart to get her walking, talking promo-dream offside this early. She needed to appear a tad friendlier, more approachable.

Unsure if what she was about to do was the right thing or a huge mistake, she rifled through her purse and handed him a business card. 'Or, here's my mobile. You can contact me on that number if you need anything.'

As long as it wasn't a triple choc-fudge sundae in the middle of the night!

'Thank you. I appreciate it.'

Natasha returned his smile, knowing he was only being polite but unable to shake the deep-seated niggle that there was more to this prince's charade than met the eye—and she'd just handed him an easy way to involve her in it!

## CHAPTER THREE

'YOU'RE late.'

Ella tapped her watch and sent a mock glower Natasha's way as her friend rushed into Trevi's and fell into her usual seat.

'Sorry,' Natasha said, unable to stop a smile spreading across her face.

She'd never been any good at keeping gossip involving guys from her best friend and, considering the afternoon she'd had, starting with meeting Dante and ending in agreeing to assist his clandestine plans, she knew this would be another one of those times where she couldn't help but share. Every last juicy detail…

'No, you're not.' Ella grinned and gestured for Luigi, their favourite waiter, to bring them the usual. 'You've got that look that says you've been up to no good. And enjoying it way too much.'

Natasha laughed and threw her hands up in

surrender. 'Give me a chance to catch my breath! And remind me to never try and hide anything from you. What are you anyway—the secret police?'

Ella pounced as soon as the words left her mouth. 'Ah! So you do have a secret! Come on, tell all.'

'Can't I at least wait till my mocha-cappuccino arrives?'

'No!' Ella shouted, and Luigi's head snapped up from the coffee machine, an indulgent smile on his face as he winked at his two favourite customers. Though Natasha suspected he said that to all the girls.

Natasha usually enjoyed toying with Ella, feeding her tiny titbits of gossip gleaned from her varied and unusual jobs in the hotel. However, by the avaricious gleam in Ella's eyes, she knew now wasn't one of those times to tease. Besides, she had the strangest urge to blurt the whole truth out and get her friend's point of view.

'Okay. Though what I'm about to say must adhere strictly to our lips-zipped policy, right?'

'Absolutely,' Ella said, miming a quick-lock zip over her lips and throwing away the key. 'It's nothing serious, is it?'

'No, everything's fine.'

She'd make sure of it.

There was no way she'd ever burden her friend with her financial troubles or the fact she could lose her home if the Towers went under.

Ella snapped her fingers. 'I know! It has something to do with the prince. How did it go? Has he swept you off your feet? Does he want to take you back to his castle and make you his love slave? Should I buy you some of those funky princess slippers?'

Natasha laughed, more than a little disturbed that Ella's preposterous questions elicited a thrill of excitement. What would it be like to be swept off her feet by a prince and spirited away to his castle to live happily ever after like the fairytales promised?

*Something you'll never know about,* her voice of reason screeched, and even the small romantic part of her that had survived Clay's treachery, the part that still harboured dreams of finding the elusive 'one' despite what she'd been through, had to agree.

'You can hold off on the slippers,' Natasha said, watching Ella lean forward with an avid look on her face. 'I don't think I'm the prince's type.'

'But you're gorgeous! You could have any man you want.' Ella's indignant quick-fire response brought an unexpected lump to Natasha's throat.

Ella had stuck by her through dating disasters, the Clay fiasco and her mum's death. She was loyal, fierce and beautiful inside and out.

'Thanks, but I think the prince has other fish to fry, so to speak. He's going incognito for a week and has asked me to keep his identity a secret. He's checked in under a false name, is parading around like an unshaven lout, and is determined to keep his true identity under wraps.'

'Wow.' Ella's eyes widened, digesting the interesting news before her razor-sharp mind predictably focussed elsewhere. 'Unshaven lout? I thought you said he looked pretty uptight.'

'I was wrong.'

Very wrong.

An instant image of dazzling blue eyes, day-old stubble, tousled dark curls and a sexy smile flashed across her mind.

'Uptight' didn't begin to describe what she thought of Dante.

Unfortunately, some of what she was thinking must've shown on her face for Ella leaned closer and patted her forearm. 'Okay, spill it. You've given me the official lips-zipped version. Now, tell me more about this prince. Is he hot?'

Natasha smiled at Ella, who was an expert at

picking up on nuances especially when they had anything to do with the male species.

She could've avoided the question, danced around it or made up a whole heap of boring platitudes. Instead, Natasha sat back and fanned her face with a red-and-white checked serviette.

'He's hot.'

Ella's eyebrows shot up in a familiar sassy look that demanded the whole truth and nothing but the truth. 'How hot?'

Natasha stopped fanning her face, threw the serviette on the table and tapped her lips as if deep in thought when, in reality, she didn't need time to ascertain how hot Dante was.

She'd known the minute he'd strutted into the lobby, all six-feet-plus of testosterone-filled male with the body of a Greek god and the face of a model.

'Tash, you're killing me here,' Ella said, her tone implicit with warning that, if Natasha didn't spill soon, she'd drag it out of her.

'Hang onto your latte, I'm trying to get my adjectives right. After all, how many ways can you say bad-boy babe with a smile that can make your knees wobble at twenty paces, and eyes that could melt a maiden aunt?'

'He's that good?'

Natasha nodded, heat seeping into her

cheeks at the memory of Dante's eyes staring at her over their espressos, an unfathomable expression in the true-blue depths. 'Better.'

Ella squealed and clapped her hands. 'This is fabulous.'

'What's fabulous?'

'This is the first time I've heard you notice a guy in months, let alone sing his praises,' Ella said, a genuinely pleased smile on her face. 'You usually pretend guys don't exist, or criticise my dates to hell and back, which is usually totally accurate by the way. Men can be scum. But this is fabulous. You're into this guy. Who cares if he's a prince? Time for you to have a little fun.'

Natasha frowned, dread creeping through her. If she was negative about guys, she had reason to be. Clay had used her, hurt her and left a lasting legacy which still threatened those she loved the most. She couldn't help the protective barriers she'd erected around her heart, but was she as bad as Ella made her sound?

Usually she would've laughed it off, but maybe her friend had a point. Perhaps she'd sounded like a shrew the last few years? As for Ella's other observation, that she was 'into' Dante, nothing could be further from the truth.

'I'm not planning on having fun with the prince,' Natasha said, ignoring her dormant devilish side which insisted it would be a blast to try. 'He has asked me for a favour, that's it. Once this week is over, I'm going to ask him for one and milk his presence in the hotel for all it's worth.'

Ella grinned. 'You don't think you're protesting just a tad too hard?'

'No!'

Okay, so that had come out a bit too defensive. Natasha forced a smile and said, 'Give it a break, will you? I've given you your gossip fix for the day, so lay off. Can't a girl enjoy her mocha-cappa in peace?'

As if on cue, Luigi bore down on their table bearing a tray filled with steaming mugs.

'*Ciao, bambinas.* How are my favourite girls today?'

He grinned broadly and placed the usual skinny latte in front of Ella and Natasha's mocha-cappuccino directly into her outstretched hands. She needed the creamy blend of chocolate and coffee desperately. The earlier espresso with Dante had barely touched the sides; besides, she'd been too engrossed in listening to His Royal Sneakiness.

Ella batted her eyelashes in the usual semi-flirtation she carried on with most men. 'We're fine, Luigi. And you?'

The Italian, old enough to be her father, kissed his fingertips and threw his hand into the air. 'All the better for seeing you, *bella*. Now, would you girls like anything else? Maybe some of my best tiramisu? Or better yet, you stay for dinner?'

'We're right for now, thanks,' Ella said, her bold smile sending the old guy into another fit of finger-kissing, hand-throwing and wistful grinning.

After Luigi had left, Natasha shook her head. 'I swear you must've come out flirting with the doctors when you were born.'

Ella shrugged, a self-satisfied smirk playing about her glossed mouth. 'Hey, if you've got it, flaunt it. Besides, the old guy loves it. And what better way to ensure we keep getting the best coffees this side of Carlton, huh?'

Natasha chuckled and took another mouth-watering sip of her mocha-coffee blend. 'You're a menace.'

'And you are changing the subject. Is there anything else about this prince I should know?' Ella took a healthy slurp of her latte and sighed with pleasure.

'No.'

Though, try as hard as she could, Natasha

couldn't dispel the memory of Dante's intense gaze as she'd handed over her card and he'd locked stares with her, his holding more than a hint of challenge. 'The prince will go about his business, I'll go about mine.'

'We talking about funny business, here?' Ella winked, and Natasha rolled her eyes before burying her twitching smile behind her giant mug.

'No, I'm not interested, and besides he's a prince,' Natasha said, amused by Ella's shenanigans despite herself.

'And?'

'And nothing.'

Natasha's response had a hollow ring to it and she knew it. However she wanted to explain it away, however she wanted to dress it up, the bizarre exchange with Dante hadn't been 'nothing'.

Dante was something.

Way too much something for her peace of mind.

'I'll let you finish your mocha,' Ella said, smiling at Natasha like a co-conspirator before spoiling the effect with, 'I'm sure you'll keep me posted about your stud-muffin prince.'

'He's not my prince!'

However, as the words left Natasha's

mouth, she wondered what the stab of disappointment was about.

Natasha had just stepped out of the shower and slipped into a fluffy purple bathrobe when her mobile rang. She considered ignoring it, as she had a date with a thriller DVD and a super-size bowl of her favourite choc-fudge ice-cream.

However, it could be her dad calling from Perth.

*Or it could be the prince.*

She wavered for a few seconds, hoping for the former, knowing a quick glance at call display would put her out of her misery. The phone continued to shrill its funky tune, and she finally gave up, crossing the room and grabbing it out of her bag.

She didn't know the number.

Punching the answer button, she put on her best phone voice, the one Ella said could scare an army into battle.

'Natasha Telford speaking.'

'Natasha, Dante here. I need your help. Urgently.'

She swallowed, surprised by the quick thrill of pleasure at the sound of his deep voice, annoyed that the movie and ice-cream would have to wait.

'What's up?'

'I'm being followed. Can you meet me out the front of the hotel in two minutes?'

Okay, so this was slightly crazy. What did he expect her to do—pull some bad-cop routine on his stalker, who was probably some lovesick girl anyway?

Shaking her head, she said, 'I'll be there.'

'Thanks, hurry,' he said, hanging up and leaving her staring at the phone.

'Drama prince!' she muttered, pulling on underwear, sweatpants and a hoodie in record time, slipping her feet into flip-flops and keys into her pocket.

She pulled her hair into a dripping ponytail as she rode the lift down to Ground, making it out the front of the hotel with thirty seconds to spare, and in time to see Dante strolling around the corner as if he didn't have a care in the world.

'So where's the fire?' she said, before he strode straight up to her, enfolded her into his arms and planted his lips on hers.

Nuts.

Insane.

Crazy.

However, as his warm, firm lips plied her with a skill she'd expect from a guy like him, her initial reaction that he'd lost his mind was quickly replaced by heat.

Burning, scorching, intense heat which raced through her body and promised to consume her from the inside out, the kind of heat that could make a girl lose her mind and do something completely out of character, like kiss him back.

Before she could react, he broke the kiss and murmured, 'Sorry, go with me for now.'

He didn't leave her much choice as he resumed kissing her, his arms sliding around her waist and feeling way too good, his chest pressed up against hers as one of his hands strummed her back like a virtuoso.

Natasha prided herself on her logic. She was a thinker, weighing up options carefully, always doing the right thing.

Then what on earth was she doing responding to the prince's passion, the heat crackling between them turning to bone-melting sizzle, enjoying this kiss more than she could've dreamed possible?

Someone moaned—to her endless embarrassment, she had a sneaking suspicion it was her—and she clung to him, belatedly realising that his rock-hard chest felt as good beneath her splayed palms as it looked.

Her senses reeled as he deepened the kiss to

the point where she could've forgotten who she was, where she was and all the reasons she shouldn't be doing this, if it wasn't for one small intrusion.

'Natasha?'

Her head snapped back and her shocked gaze swung between Dante, the prince who'd just lost his mind and kissed her senseless, and Clay, the man she'd once loved and now despised.

# CHAPTER FOUR

'WHAT are you doing here?'

Natasha glared at Clay, hating the perfection of his smooth blond hair gelled within an inch of its life, the supercilious sneer, the cocky squared shoulders ready for battle.

She loathed him.

She despised him.

Yet she'd once loved him with all her heart.

Thank goodness she'd had a wake-up call before she'd made the biggest mistake of her life. Being engaged to the pompous ass had ruined her family as it was. She shuddered to think what would've happened if she'd gone all the way.

But then, she already knew.

The scumbag had told her in great detail when she'd broken off their engagement after learning the truth about why a suave entrepreneur was really interested in marrying a hotel jill of all trades.

'Guess there's no need to ask you,' Clay said, sending her a look that could kill. 'It's pretty obvious you've taken up sport since we parted. Tonsil hockey.'

'Leave the lady alone,' Dante said, his voice low with menace, a protective arm still wrapped around her waist, and Natasha instinctively snuggled deeper before realising what she was doing. By then, she didn't want to move. Having his arm holding her, supporting her, felt way too good in the face of Clay's derision.

Clay's withering gaze turned on Dante. 'And I must've been mistaken about you. I thought you were the Prince of Calida back there, but guess I was wrong.'

'You got that right,' Dante said, his hand tightening on her waist.

Natasha stiffened, knowing how much Dante's privacy meant, and what a louse like Clay would do with the information if he found out. Guys like Clay did everything for a reason, which usually involved getting ahead in the world and looking out for number one.

'Instead, you're Natasha's new boyfriend. How sweet.'

There was nothing remotely sweet about the false saccharine dripping from Clay's every word or the nasty leer he turned on her. 'I should've known. There's no way a prince would be remotely interested in someone like you.'

Natasha flinched despite the shield she'd built around her ego after ending the relationship with Clay.

Damn him, for still having the power to hurt her.

Damn him, for being here and potentially ruining her plan to use the prince to salvage something from the mess he'd lumbered her family with.

'Apologise to the lady. Now.'

Dante's arm slipped from her waist as he took a step forward and, crazily, she missed its solid warmth.

Clay's sneer turned sinister, the same expression she'd seen eighteen months ago when she'd told him what he could do with his two-carat baguette diamond.

'And who are you to give me orders?' Clay matched Dante's step forward till the two were almost toe to toe.

Natasha laid a steadying hand on Dante's arm, shocked that she noticed how hot his bare skin felt under her palm and how much she liked it.

'He's someone you'll never be,' she said, wishing she'd had the guts to inject this much scorn into her voice the last time they'd spoken, when he'd threatened her family yet again. 'Now get lost.'

Clay's eyes narrowed to slits, reminding her of a snake she'd once seen at Australia's biggest reptile park: dangerous, slimy, lethal.

'You'll be sorry,' he said, so softly she could've imagined it.

However, Dante's bunched forearm muscles under her hand told her she hadn't. He was wound tighter than a spring, and looked ready to defend her honour whether she needed it or not.

As much as she liked his chivalry, she didn't need an international incident on her hotel's doorstep. Besides, Clay wasn't worth it. He wasn't worth anything as far as she was concerned.

Not any more.

'First you don't apologise, now you're threatening the lady? Who the hell do you think you are?'

Dante had shrugged off her restraining hand and now stood in Clay's face, while Natasha struggled between leaping on Dante's back to distract him and slugging Clay herself.

'I was the fool who was going to marry her,' Clay said, casting one last malevolent glare her way before turning on his heel and walking off.

Clay's cowardice shouldn't have surprised

her. Nothing about him surprised her, considering what he'd put her through, what he'd put her whole family through.

Dante turned to face her, incredulity lending his handsome face a comical look. 'You were engaged to that slime?'

'Don't remind me.'

She held up her hand as if trying to ward off any further talk of Clay. Needless to say, a smart guy like Dante didn't buy it for a second.

'You can do so much better than him.'

Dante spoke softly, his blue eyes warm, a tentative smile flirting around his mouth as he reached out and captured both her hands.

Natasha had expected him to interrogate her, to question her lousy judgement, to do any number of things apart from what he was doing now—holding her hands with a gentle tenderness that brought a lump to her throat.

She stared at their linked hands, enjoying the solid warmth they provided, a comfort which she'd never got from the few times Clay would deign to be touched in public.

*Reality check—the guy is a prince. A prince you need to save your business. A prince who needs his identity protected, yet here you are getting all mushy with him out the front of your hotel.*

Disengaging her hands from his, she folded her arms over her chest. 'So what was the urgent business?' *And what on earth was all that amazing kissing about?*

Though she wisely kept that question to herself for now. She needed to reassemble her wits before she tackled him over his lip-lock, considering her resistance was at an all-time low following his whole knight-in-shining-armour impersonation.

'That idiot was following me. He called out "prince" several times but I ignored him. I wanted you to meet me out the front so you could pretend to be my girlfriend and throw him off the track.'

He had the grace to look sheepish. 'I didn't know he was your ex. I'm sorry about that.'

Okay, so that explained his over-zealous welcome when he'd first seen her outside the hotel. But darn it, his kisses had seemed so real…

Giving herself a mental shake, Natasha tilted her chin up and glared at Dante. 'Pretty stupid plan.'

He shrugged, looking more adorable than guilty or apologetic with that sexy smile tugging at the corners of his mouth. 'It was all I could think of on the spur of the moment. I can't let anyone know who I am. You know that, it's too important to me.'

Natasha stifled a snort. Too important to his floozy, more like.

'When I gave you my number for emergencies, I didn't expect...' She trailed off, not wanting to bring up the sizzling kisses, knowing it couldn't be ignored. 'This,' she finished lamely, waving a hand between the two of them.

'You mean the way I kissed you?'

With a glint in his eyes, his gaze dropped to her lips, which tingled at the memory of his wonderful technique, how he'd made her forget every worry she had.

'Yes, that.'

Heat seeped into her cheeks, scorching with embarrassment. It wasn't so much the fact he'd kissed her but how she'd responded, like a woman who enjoyed it. Way too much. And she had an awful suspicion he knew that.

'Like I said, a spur of the moment thing, an impulse,' he said, a hint of laughter in his voice. 'I apologise if it wasn't right.'

'Oh, no, it was fine,' she blurted, before clamping her lips shut in horror.

He'd meant it wasn't the right thing to do; she'd responded about his technique. Could the ground just open up and swallow her now—please?

Thankfully, he didn't call her on her monstrous gaff. He just stood there, looking way too sexy with his smile, his tousled hair and those gorgeous blue eyes sparkling with humour.

'Thank you for rescuing me,' he said, giving her another of those quaint little bows that must have been standard for royalty in Calida. 'Shall we retire?'

Natasha nodded and managed a sedate 'Uh-huh,' before she made a total ass of herself and took his question as an invitation to go up to his room and tuck his royal pain-in-the-butt in.

As they entered the elaborate lobby, and she caught site of herself in the huge ornate mirrors lining the pillars, Natasha stifled a groan. Grey sweatpants, a pale blue hoodie and navy beaded flip-flops did little to accentuate her make-upless face and wet ponytail.

She looked like a bedraggled waif next to a tanned god, and for a split second chastised herself for wishing things were different, annoyed that she cared.

Forgetting his royal status, she wondered what would it be like to stroll into a hotel with a guy like Dante by her side? A guy who protected his woman, a guy who looked like every woman's walking talking fantasy, a guy who could kiss like the prince in a fairy tale?

'In your dreams!' she muttered, grateful when the lifts came into sight.

'Pardon?'

She forced a tight smile. 'Goodnight.'

'Sleep well,' Dante murmured, planting a quick kiss on her cheek before she could move. 'And thank you once again.'

Natasha whirled on her heel and entered the lift for the apartments, her cheek tingling, her emotions in turmoil. She waited till she heard the zing of the lift for the hotel before turning around, hitting the button for her own floor and sinking against the side wall, grateful for the support.

She needed it. With her head spinning from encountering Clay, kissing Dante and the pathetic way she'd tied herself up in knots, she was a mess.

Definitely time for that choc-fudge ice-cream. Though, after the last half hour she'd had, nothing less than the tub would do now.

# CHAPTER FIVE

DANTE shrugged out of his leather jacket, tossed it on the bed and headed for the bathroom. He needed a shower, a cold punishing shower, considering what he'd just done.

*You didn't play fair,* he muttered to his unshaven reflection in the huge mirror above an equally large marble basin as he braced himself against it.

Then again, who'd said anything about playing?

Adjusting the mixer, he splashed icy water on his face and dabbed it with a baby-soft towel which smelt like freshly squeezed lemons. Only the best for Telford Towers. And that extended to its stunning stand-in concierge who took her job to extremes.

He shouldn't have kissed Natasha.

He knew that.

She knew that.

But he'd gone ahead and done it anyway, giving her some lousy excuse about using her as his girlfriend to put that crazy jerk who'd been following him off the track.

He'd had it all worked out: get her to meet him out the front of the hotel, slip a casual arm around her shoulders, give her a quick peck on the cheek and stroll to the nearest café like they'd intended on meeting all along.

Instead, the minute he'd caught sight of her, all fresh faced and righteously indignant, his plans for a quick peck had taken on a life of their own and he'd swept her into his arms before he could think twice.

At least the ruse had worked.

But at what cost?

He'd sensed a connection between Natasha and her ex, some unfinished business. Unresolved feelings, perhaps?

If he'd jeopardised something for her, he should feel bad. Instead, the thought of that supercilious creep anywhere near the petite brunette made him want to order a royal head-lopping—if they still went in for that sort of thing in the twenty-first century.

The jerk had been rude, arrogant and condescending, and he couldn't see a feisty woman like Natasha putting up with him. Then again, what did he know about women? His sister Gina was driving him mad, and his mother would have him married off the second he stepped back on Calida.

Speaking of Gina, the way Natasha had handled the situation earlier could make her the perfect candidate for what he had in mind. After today, Dante couldn't handle Gina and her idiosyncrasies alone, that much was clear.

He needed the help of a woman, a very astute woman.

Thankfully, he had a good feeling that Natasha could be just what he was looking for.

Natasha sipped at her mocha-cappuccino and strode towards Telford Towers, unable to hide a proud smile behind her styrofoam mug. With the early morning sun tipping the sandstone turrets in pale gold, the cloudless blue sky framing the impressive façade and the gleaming windows, the place looked incredible.

It looked like home.

The only home she'd ever known.

*Yeah, for how much longer?*

Her smile vanished and she took another gulp of coffee, knowing the bitter aftertaste had nothing to do with caffeine and everything to do with Clay and his treachery.

The guy was pure evil and, the sooner she made the final two payments and got him out of their lives for good, the sooner she could rest easy.

Seeing him yesterday had resurrected too many painful memories: of how gullible and stupid she'd been to fall for his smooth lines and good looks. But it had been more than that.

Having Dante look at her with confusion that she could've been associated with a creep like Clay had affected her more than lousy memories. She didn't like looking a fool. She wanted him to see her as cool, collected and capable. After all, why else would he want to be associated with her hotel?

She'd cursed fate when she'd learned the truth about Clay and their engagement, and it looked like fate still liked to grab hold of her leg and yank hard. Only problem was, she wasn't laughing.

And she hoped Dante wouldn't think her a complete moron for ever looking twice at a guy like Clay.

Finishing off the last of the coffee, she tossed the mug in a bin and headed for the front of the hotel. She had five minutes before her shift started, and she wanted to have a quick chat with the night concierge before handover.

However, like most of her intentions these days, it wasn't meant to be.

'Can I have a word?'

Dante stepped from the shadows of an ornate column near the hotel's entrance, and she had no option but to stop. Either that or fob off her big chance to save the hotel once and for all.

'Sure, but I don't have long,' she said, fixing a polite smile on her face, hoping her surprise didn't show.

For royalty, this guy had the whole casual thing down pat. Dark denim, khaki T-shirt, boat shoes. Throw in the mussed hair and designer stubble, and he looked like he'd just strolled in from a dawn sail on the bay—wind-ruffled, tousled and sexy. Very, very sexy.

'This won't take long.'

He laid a hand in the small of her back and propelled her to a quiet spot behind a towering flower pot.

'If this is about last night, don't worry about it. I'm not.'

*Yeah, right.* That's why she'd guzzled a half-carton of ice-cream, missed most of the best thriller released this year and spent half the night tossing and turning over the way he'd kissed her.

'Actually, this has got something to do with last night.'

He rubbed a hand over his face, a strangely weary gesture for a guy who had it all.

'I was very impressed with how you handled the situation, and I was wondering if you'd consider being my temporary PA for the next week?'

'What?'

Okay, so the whole jaw-dropping thing wouldn't look too good, but for a minute there she could've sworn His Royal Scruffiness had asked her to be his PA?

'I know it sounds crazy, but the family business I need to take care of is a lot more complicated than I first thought. I need help and that's where you come in. If you'll agree, that is.'

He smiled, a beguiling, seductive grin that could've coerced an ice-cream addict to part with her last scoop. Totally unfair.

'So, you do have family business?'

Oops; her first thought slipped out before she could stop it and she hoped he'd gloss over it. *As if.*

'Of course. That's what I told you before.'

A tiny frown marred the almost too-perfect rugged face before a spark of enlightenment flashed in his eyes.

'You didn't believe me.'

'No…yes…of course I did,' she blustered on like a moron, a growing blush adding to her embarrassment.

What was it about this guy that tied her up in knots? She'd handled VIPs her whole life and had never been this flustered, this out of control.

Okay, so most of those guys had looked like the back end of a Melbourne tram, but that didn't mean anything. It wasn't Dante's sexy looks that had her flustered—well, not much anyway—but more to do with the way he made her feel: valued, important, someone he could depend on.

'No, you didn't. What did you think I was doing here a week earlier than my official business?'

Natasha took a steadying breath. Ella often accused her of being brutally frank but now wasn't a time to be honest.

'Well, I thought you might've had other friends to visit, apart from family, that is.'

*Hmm…not a bad save.*

'You thought I had some secret mistress hidden away somewhere, didn't you?'

Not a bad save…a terrible one! He hadn't bought her fluffed explanation for a second. So the guy wasn't just a pretty face. Couldn't he have some flaws?

When in doubt, Natasha reverted to type and went on the offensive.

'Mistress? You sound like you've stepped out of the seventeenth century. I didn't think you royal types would use terminology like that any more.'

She sent an obvious glance at her watch, implying she had more important things to do, like start work, rather than stand here and feel like a fool.

For that's exactly what she was, a big fool, making assumptions about a guy she didn't know and solely based on his royal status and incredible looks.

'You don't think much of me, do you?'

His clear blue eyes narrowed, watching her, assessing her, probably judging her, just as she'd judged him.

She stiffened, hating that her plan to smooth things over after last night's fiasco was going horribly awry.

'I don't know you.'

He paused, his face inscrutable, before the corners of his mouth twitched. 'Well, we'll just have to remedy that, won't we? And what better way than have you help me out as my PA for the next week?'

'You're crazy. I have a job, remember? And speaking of which…' She tapped her watch face and sent a pointed glance over his shoulder. 'The concierge will be late if you don't let me go.'

'I'd only need a few hours of your time each day. Maybe after your shift? I promise it won't be difficult. I just need someone with local knowledge of Melbourne, and I think you'd be perfect. From what I've seen, you can handle anything.'

His lips curved into a knowing smile, the type of smile that implied he knew exactly how he'd affected her last night with those scintillating kisses, whether they'd been part of a mock charade or not.

'You will be handsomely reimbursed.'

Natasha refrained from snorting. *Handsomely reimbursed.* Despite his scruffy appearance, he really did sound like a pompous... pompous...*prince* at times!

'I don't need your money.'

However, as soon as the words flew out of her mouth, she knew it was a lie. The hotel did need the money. Though Dante couldn't offer her anywhere near the kind of money that would come close to clearing her debts.

Suddenly, inspiration struck. She needed what his reputation could bring to the hotel— the prestige, the raised profile, the fame would send bookings through the roof—and she'd intended on approaching him for help at the end of this week.

But what about right now? The way she saw it, a perfect exchange: her help with his mysterious 'family business' in exchange for his princely profile once he came out of the royal closet at the end of the week.

She couldn't lose.

'I won't take your money, but I think we could come to some other sort of arrangement,' she said, hoping he'd go for her idea.

Rather than looking surprised, his eyes glittered with intrigue as he leaned towards her, enveloping her in a sensual cloud of fresh air, the citrus soap the hotel favoured and pure Dante. Intoxicating, heady and totally addictive…if she lost her mind!

'What sort of arrangement did you have in mind?' His low, husky voice rippled over her, making her feel more woman than she ever had in all the clinches with Clay.

'Not that sort!'

She stepped back and held her hands up, as if trying to ward him off. This guy was seriously dangerous to her peace of mind. She should be telling him what to do with his PA offer and running a hundred miles in the opposite direction.

However, she didn't have an option. She'd

plain run out of options around the time she'd landed her family in this mess in the first place.

Dante was the answer to her problems. All she had to do was get her overactive imagination under control and she'd be fine. Telford Towers would be fine. Her family wouldn't lose the business that meant everything to them, and her friends and employees wouldn't be homeless and jobless.

She could do this.

She had to.

'The hotel needs to raise its profile, and I was hoping after your week of going incognito is over you wouldn't mind me advertising the fact of your presence here. Perhaps take part in some promotions?'

The sensual glitter vanished in a second, his eyes turning a cold, hard, arctic blue. 'Fine.'

Though he didn't look fine. In fact, he looked like she'd just insulted him.

'Look, if you're not comfortable—'

'I said it's fine. Your help in exchange for mine. Now, what time do you finish?'

'Three.'

'I'll meet you in the lobby at three-thirty.' He sent her a brief, dismissive nod, and she knew exactly how his army of servants must feel back in his homeland.

'Okey dokey,' she muttered, casting a confused glance his way before heading inside.

However, she'd barely made it past him when he stopped her with a hand on her arm. She stared at his hand: the long, elegant fingers, the clean, blunt fingernails, and the smooth tanned skin. The type of hand that had never done a day's manual labour in its life, the type of hand used to the best manicures and people fawning over it—the type of hand she should scorn but couldn't, when its barest touch sent her pulse tripping.

'Thank you,' he said, so softly she had to lean forward to hear it, giving her another whopping dose of his heady scent.

'No worries.'

She managed a tight smile before slipping out of his grasp and heading into the hotel.

No worries indeed…

# CHAPTER SIX

AFTER slipping into black denim hipsters, a funky red top and pulling her hair free of its constricting chignon she usually wore for work, Natasha barely had time to run a brush through her kinky hair and slick gloss over her lips before rushing out to meet Dante.

'Hey, where's the fire? Or, more to the point, where's the fireman?' Ella wolf whistled as the lift doors slid open and Natasha all but tumbled in.

'I've got a meeting,' Natasha said, avoiding Ella's inquisitive stare as she smoothed her hair in the mirror over the lift buttons.

'With anyone I know?'

Ella's silky tone told Natasha her best friend knew exactly where she was going and who she was meeting.

'Dante and I have some business to discuss.'

'I just bet you do.'

Ella made childish puckering noises and Natasha rolled her eyes.

'So, how's it going with the bad boy formerly known as prince?'

Natasha chuckled at her friend's joke. 'Not bad. He's actually an okay sort of guy.'

'I know, I know.' Ella made mock fanning motions in front of her face. 'I saw him in the lobby today. And, let me tell you, okay doesn't begin to describe that guy!'

'He is pretty hot, isn't he?'

Okay, so she was only human. She could admit the obvious without letting the fact turn her head.

'Hot?' Ella's voice shot up five octaves. 'The guy is drop-dead gorgeous! Pity about the royal stuff, because he'd be perfect for you.'

'What makes you say that?'

Ella knew she'd been through hell with Clay, though she didn't know the half of it or why Natasha so desperately needed Dante's co-operation. Ella knew she rarely dated and how she'd totally lost trust in guys. So what made her think some prince she barely knew would be perfect for her?

'Oh…just something he said.'

Ella studied her chipped fingernails at arm's length, trying to stifle a cheeky grin and losing.

'What did you do?'

Natasha's heart sank to the soles of her high-heeled black boots. Though she loved Ella dearly, subtlety wasn't one of her friend's strong suits. And if she'd said something to Dante…*help*!

'Nothing.' Ella widened her blue eyes, aiming for a guileless look and failing miserably.

'Ella!'

'Okay, okay. All I did was ask him if he'd seen the concierge because I needed to ask you something, and he got this goofy look on his face when he glanced over at your desk. That's it, I swear.'

'You sure?'

'Positive.'

'Stay out of this, El,' Natasha said, as the lift slid to a smooth stop and the steel doors opened. 'I mean it,' she added as Ella opened her mouth to respond.

'Spoilsport,' Ella muttered as she brushed past her, twirling to a stop when they exited the lift, waiting for the doors to close on a large group of Japanese tourists. 'Enjoy your *meeting*.'

Natasha resisted the urge to poke her tongue out at Ella's retreating back. She didn't expect a bit of imaginary matchmaking from Ella, who was usually totally pragmatic, even if she did flirt with every guy lucky enough to enter her sphere.

The only goofy look Ella must've seen on Dante's face was the same look Natasha had got this morning when she'd proposed he help her with promoting the hotel. Now that suggestion had gone down a treat—not.

His frigid expression had been pure royal, a cold reaction used to snub people who didn't please him, and entirely at odds with his casual appearance. He might try to play down his royal blood for the week with laid-back clothes and ruffled hair, but she knew better. Guys like him were used to being obeyed, used to things going their way, and he probably hadn't liked being trumped by an upstart like her.

What did he think, she'd help him purely out of the goodness of her heart?

Yeah, right. She'd tried that once before and look where it had landed her: neck-deep in financial trouble.

She'd been gullible, trusting and sweet at one time. Not any more.

Dante had something she wanted and vice versa.

She just hoped she wouldn't confuse exactly what it was she wanted from him.

* * *

'You want my help with *what*?'

Natasha stared at Dante like he'd just asked her to strip naked and dance down Bourke Street.

He shrugged, a sheepish expression on his way-too-handsome face, managing to look needy and gorgeous at the same time. 'You live in Melbourne. You'd know where all the best toy stores are and who I can hire to organise the best party.'

'For a two-year-old?'

She shook her head and blew her fringe out of her eyes. She should've stuck with the chignon. That way, she could've taken out the pin holding it up and stabbed him with it.

'It's hard work. I spent the whole day traipsing around your city yesterday and came up with nothing. I have a few days to get this party organized, and I don't know where to start.'

'Then why did you take it on?'

His eyes glittered with emotion and she swallowed her next sarcastic question about what an Italian prince would know about kiddie parties.

'My sister is a scatterbrain. She isn't the most organised person in the world, and by what I've seen so far planning stuff like birthday parties isn't her forte. I want Paolo to have a special day.'

A day he probably wouldn't remember when

he was older, but Natasha kept that gem to herself too.

So the guy had a good heart. She couldn't fault him for caring about his nephew. But a kid's party? She knew as much about organising that as she did abseiling. Absolutely nothing.

'Think you can do it?'

She met his challenging gaze head-on, knowing she'd make this work if she had to don a clown costume and take a crash course in juggling herself.

This was too important.

Getting Dante's reciprocal help at the end of the week was vital.

Tilting her head up, she said, 'You bet. Let's get started.'

'I knew I could count on you.'

He smiled, just another of his regular run-of-the-mill smiles which made her feel like she was the only woman in the world. Obviously a part of his Prince Charming act, something he used to coerce people to bend to his will on a daily basis, but boy did those curving lips pack a power punch!

'First up, we'll need to surf the Net, come up with a concise list. It'll save us loads of time. Then I'll narrow down the choices with your help and check out our options.'

'Very efficient.'

'Okay, then. I'll get to it.'

He arched an eyebrow, the imperious prince questioning a serf's insubordination, and she stifled a smile at the analogy.

'I thought we'd be working on this together?'

Oh no. He'd thought wrong. Spending one-on-one time with the gorgeous prince, work or not, wouldn't be good. He awakened feelings in her she'd rather suppress. Feelings of being appreciated and, worse, feeling like he saw her as a woman, an attractive woman, and she wouldn't go there. She couldn't. She'd done it before with a smooth, handsome charmer and her battered self-esteem was still recovering.

'I don't need you.'

*Ouch!* That came out a lot harsher than she'd intended and she bit her lip, wishing he didn't make her feel so gauche, so out of her depth.

'You sure about that?'

A teasing glint lighting his eyes, he leaned forward a centimetre. It felt much closer, like he'd infused her personal space with too much manly presence, and she was grateful that they hadn't left the lobby yet.

'Positive.'

Her less than emphatic nod did little to

convince him, given his lips curved upwards in a knowing smile.

'Look, I want your help, but I need to be involved in this too. That's the whole point of me coming out here a week earlier and going through this ruse. I wanted to make this special for Paolo, to get to know my nephew, and I can't do that if I delegate all the work to you. I'd hoped we'd work as a team, you coming up with the information I need, me having enough input to feel like I'm not a totally useless uncle breezing through on a fly-by-night official visit.'

The anti-men shield surrounding Natasha's heart cracked just a fraction at his declaration. Who couldn't like a guy for wanting the best for his little nephew?

If only Dante could be more uppity, more demanding, more…princely! That way, she could despise him for his airs and keep him at arm's length. As it was she found him too attractive, and now with this softer side she had a sinking feeling he could undermine her carefully erected defences all too easily.

She didn't like trusting men.

She didn't like opening herself up to feeling like a fool.

And she sure didn't like her self-esteem taking another swan dive when she admitted that the only reason a guy like Dante paid any attention to her was because of what she could do for him.

'Okay. I'll get my laptop and meet you back here. We can grab a coffee at one of the nearby trattorias while we work.'

'Perfect,' he said, pinning her with an intense stare that made her wish for a host of crazy things: that his husky 'perfect' referred to her, that her not-so-perfect persona was willing to take a chance on having a little fun, and that maybe, just maybe, she could shrug off the weight of familial responsibility weighing down her shoulders and live a little today without thinking about tomorrow.

'Back in a sec.'

She turned and managed to walk to the lift with all the finesse of a runway model, minus the hip swivels those girls had down pat. However, she couldn't shake the feeling Dante watched her every step, and when she risked a quick glance over her shoulder before stepping into the lift, which thankfully appeared sooner rather than later, he raised his hand in a brief wave.

She stumbled into the lift and hit the button for her floor, leaning on the cool steel wall for support.

So much for poise.

It wasn't his wave that had undermined her cool act as much as the sexy grin which said he'd watched her fake strut to the lift and had enjoyed every minute of it.

Prince or not, saving her hotel or not, the guy was trouble.

And it looked like she'd just landed in a whole heap of it.

Dante dealt with people from all walks of life, from diplomats to prime ministers, kings to blue-collar workers. His mum said he had a gift for reading people, for knowing the right thing to say and when.

Somehow, the way the woman sitting next to him reacted every time he opened his mouth, he felt his 'gift' needed some serious re-wrapping.

'Come up with anything yet?'

She held up her hand, a tiny frown creasing her brow, giving her an utterly adorable studious look.

'Give me another minute then I'll show you what I've got.'

'Good,' he said, sitting back to finish his espresso and free to study her.

He couldn't figure her out.

She had this uptight business persona that

she wore with pride, even in her out of work hours. And though she dressed like any other fashion-loving woman in her twenties—he'd had a difficult time tearing his eyes away from the way her cute butt had filled out the black denim earlier and how that racy red top accentuated every luscious curve—she didn't act her age.

He found spontaneous, fun-loving and flirty women irresistible. Yet, Natasha didn't appear to have an impulsive bone in her sensational body. She was serious, fastidious and solemn. What would it take to get her to loosen up a little?

*Why do you care?*

He sipped his espresso, studying the way her shiny brown hair hung in a sleek curtain around her face, a deep, rich brown, the colour of Swiss chocolate, and a perfect frame for her expressive face. He wouldn't call her beautiful in the classical sense but there was something about her that was striking…the full lips, the slightly elongated nose, the large hazel eyes… Her face was memorable, and he could easily spend the next few hours staring at it.

By the serious frown she fixed him with when her gaze swung up to meet his, he guessed that wouldn't be happening.

'Okay, here's what I've come up with so far.'

She grabbed a pen and started ticking off the extensive list she'd made as she'd surfed the Net. 'We've got pony parties, Clarice the Clown, roaming reptiles, magicians, ventriloquists, go-karts, mobile animal farms, painting parties, fire engines and the old standard bouncy castles.'

She looked at him expectantly, not waiting for a response, before snapping her fingers. 'Or, if Paolo is a new-age sort of guy, there are fairies, discos and belly dancers.'

Dante shook his head. For a guy who'd hosted world summits and mastered complex budgets, he had no idea when it came to this sort of stuff. 'You discovered all that in ten minutes?'

'Uh-huh.'

Her sceptical look said it all. She obviously wondered why he hadn't jumped on a computer and done the same, and he'd be damned if he clued her in to the fact he had other people do this type of research work for him all the time.

She already seemed to have little regard for his background; there was no use emphasising the yawning gap between them.

'Well done. How about we narrow it down to about three and screen them tomorrow?'

Her eyebrows shot up. 'You want me to interview some clown?'

'No. I need you to make sure the reptiles are docile enough.'

'As if.'

She joined in his laughter, and it took every ounce of his willpower not to take advantage of the shared camaraderie of the moment and ask her what was bothering her, why the reticence.

'I want Paolo's party to be perfect, and I have full confidence you'll ensure that.'

He barely caught her muttered 'I'm glad someone has confidence in me,' as he leaned forward to get a better look at her list, rather pleased it brought him closer to her.

She wore a subtle fragrance, a light floral, which intrigued him. The smell had lingered after she'd joined in the girlfriend charade, his senses filled with the taste of her lips, the feel of her in his arms and the unique scent which enticed him to come back for more.

'Personally, for a two-year-old, I'd go with the animals or the bouncy castle. All kids like animals and have energy to burn.'

She rapped the pen against the list, studying it with great attention to detail and avoiding looking at him.

'Let's consider both possibilities tomorrow.'

He reached out and stilled her hand with his, her head snapping up as she shot him a startled look. However, she didn't pull away, and in that first loaded second when her gaze met his, he saw something which surprised him.

Pure, honest interest. A spark of something more, something bordering on desire?

It couldn't be.

He was projecting his own attraction to the sexy brunette onto her, wishing for something that wasn't there. Not that he would act on his impulse if there was. He didn't do dalliances, especially when visiting foreign countries. He'd made that mistake once before, and the ensuing publicity had dogged him for months.

'Can I borrow this? I want to make a list of possible gifts before I forget.'

He plucked the pen out of her fingers, wondering if she bought his smooth cover-up for the momentary gaff.

Touching her wasn't a good idea when looking was difficult enough.

'Sure.'

She reached for her lukewarm latte, avoiding his eyes.

Damn. So much for that camaraderie he'd imagined a few moments ago.

'I'm thinking about buying a racing-car set,

an electric train-set, a few computer games, something along those lines.'

She rolled her eyes, just as he'd expected her to at his ludicrous suggestions, but at least he'd achieved what he'd set out to do. She was looking at him again.

'You have no idea about kids, do you?'

'Not much.'

A fact which saddened him. For a carefree bachelor who knew his single days were numbered—Calida needed heirs, and it was only a matter of time before he succumbed to his mother's meddling—he wasn't so scared of losing his freedom any more, and kids were a part of that.

Not that he'd ever been free in the true sense of the word. He'd had responsibilities from the time of his birth, and with the early death of his father and his mum threatening to abdicate and hand over the reign to him any day now, he'd never been free.

'Okay. Here's what we'll do. Tomorrow after work, we'll check out the animals and the castle then we'll hit Toys R Us for some serious gift hunting. Sound like a plan?'

He nodded, enjoying her take-charge attitude. It got tiring making all the decisions all the time.

'Are you always this organised and thorough?'

She blushed and fiddled with the list, folding the paper edges into tiny creases. 'I try to be,' she said, her tone defensive.

'Relax. It was a compliment.'

'Thanks.'

She didn't look grateful. In fact, she looked downright uncomfortable, and Dante knew he had to quit while he was behind. Yet another conversation heading south with the woman he couldn't read.

And it was frustrating the hell out of him.

'Would you like to have dinner before we go back?'

He asked out of politeness, but a small part of him wished she'd accept. He never had a chance to eat like this: casually, anonymously, without a horde of people waiting for him to finish his soup or take a sip of wine before touching their own.

'Thanks, but it's been a long day.'

She gathered her papers, laptop and pens and stuffed them all into a large black bag which looked like it could carry a year's worth of hotel bathroom supplies.

'Maybe tomorrow?'

A half-hearted nod in his direction didn't inspire him with confidence, and he knew without a doubt the minute they concluded their business tomorrow night he'd get the same response.

He couldn't figure her out.

It was driving him insane.

# CHAPTER SEVEN

'So YOU won't eat with me but you'll let me buy you a drink?'

Natasha cradled her glass, swirled the full-bodied shiraz and stared into its ruby depths. Nope, no answers to her confusion there, considering she'd been wondering the same thing since they'd entered the Lobby Bar a few minutes ago.

'I usually have a nightcap before I go to bed,' she said, knowing her steaming mug of hot chocolate complete with two pink marshmallows didn't really compare to sharing a smooth red with a sexy prince.

'Really?'

He quirked an eyebrow, no doubt at the thought of her quaffing wine by herself before bed. Hmm…not the type of image she wanted to portray.

'I'm a cocoa addict,' she admitted, joining in

his laughter and ruining her sophisticated act totally. 'But this is great,' she quickly added, lifting her glass in his direction, feeling gauche and unworldly compared with his polish.

'You didn't really answer my question,' he said, fixing her with the type of stare she imagined he used on wayward inferiors.

'Maybe I didn't want to bruise your ego totally, so softened the blow of refusing dinner by sharing a wine with you?'

His startled expression had her hiding a grin behind her wine glass. She doubted His Royal Highness received many knock-backs let alone had his ego bruised too often.

In reality, she'd refused his dinner invitation because it had seemed too intimate. She was attracted enough to him without sitting across a cosy table for two for hours, giving him the opportunity to captivate her with his natural charm.

Dante made her feel like a woman and then some, the monstrous cultural gap between them disappearing when he stared at her like every word she uttered was a riveting soliloquy. Worse, he made her forget every logical reason why she was with him—to work—and that scared her beyond belief.

He shook his head, smiling. 'You're still not answering me.'

Uh-oh; it looked like she couldn't put him off. She could try flirting, which she was hopeless at, or she could fluff around and look more of a fool in the process. Or she could take the only way out she knew and be upfront.

'Honestly? I feel out of my depth around you.'

His smile disappeared in a flash, replaced by an instant frown. 'How so?'

Natasha sighed, hating her bluntness at times. How could she articulate how Dante made her feel when she barely knew herself?

'I'm not sure. I guess it's been a while since I've socialised outside of work, and I'm not so good at it any more.'

'Have I made you feel inferior in some way? Is that the problem?'

'No!'

'Would you like some time to think about that?'

Natasha chuckled. 'You're not like that. In fact, apart from the odd pompous word or two, you're nothing like what I imagined royalty to be.'

He didn't have an Italian accent, but she guessed that's because he'd gone to school in England and spent most of his schooling life there, or so his Net profile said, but he didn't speak with a plum in his mouth either. Also, his laid-back attitude surprised her, and he didn't use power like she'd assumed he would.

Unlike Clay, who'd thought nothing of belittling waiters or valets when it suited.

'Then what's the problem? It was only dinner.'

Exactly. It wasn't like he'd asked her to spend the night or anything.

Oh-oh. She didn't want to think about what spending the night with a guy like Dante would be like. If being around him had her flustered, imagining those sorts of scenarios would be enough to push her over the edge.

'Dinner seems more…casual. So far, every time we've met, it's for business and I want to keep it that way.'

'Understandable, but dinner can be business-like.'

Given the glint in his too-blue eyes and the sexy smile playing about his mouth, the last thing she would be concentrating on over dinner was business.

Natasha twirled a strand of hair around her finger, wishing she'd never opened her big mouth and gone down this track in the first place. 'Can we change the subject, please?'

He hesitated before nodding. 'I've never met a woman so honest before. It's refreshing.'

*It's suicidal*, she thought, knowing she must

look like a backward hick to a refined man of the world like him. For goodness' sake, it had been only a simple dinner invitation and she was acting like an uptight prude.

She wished she was the type of girl to flirt, have fun and then wave *bon voyage* to Dante at the end of his stay. But she wasn't. She'd never been frivolous, and her bitter experience with Clay had ruined her take-a-chance side.

Sure, Dante was gorgeous and nice and nothing like she'd expected, but she couldn't do the whole casual thing. It just wasn't her.

'You don't appreciate me talking so openly?'

'Like you, I find it refreshing. I'm not used to it.'

Clay had been a duplicitous creep, and she hated her foolishness in believing every word his lying mouth had uttered.

'You have been hurt.'

He pronounced it like a royal decree, and she wavered for a second, torn between unburdening herself and running screaming from the room.

She really shouldn't drink wine on an empty stomach; it gave her crazy ideas.

Perhaps she could move on one day and learn to trust again. Though trust a prince with the looks of a model and the glib lines of a playboy? She'd do better trusting a snake.

'Not hurt so much as had my eyes opened. The business world is tough, and Telford Towers means a lot to me. I've invested my life in the place.'

Nice save.

She'd brushed aside his personal take on her ramblings and turned it into a business one. Now maybe she could take her foot out of her mouth and turn the next few minutes into a pleasurable exchange of light-hearted conversation rather than baring her soul and sending the prince running.

She'd never done the normal dating thing other girls did, just never had the time, and it showed. Here she was, sharing a perfect shiraz with a gorgeous prince, and she was one step away from making a prize ass of herself. She really needed to get out more.

'The business world is a cut-throat one. And I can see why this hotel means so much to you.'

He raised his glass in the general direction of the mahogany woodwork and brass sconces, and she sighed in relief. He'd bought her brush-off.

'You have done a marvellous job here. I'm not surprised you agreed to my outlandish proposal if I can help you let the world know about this.'

She almost choked on her wine, clearing her throat with a few discreet coughs. If he only knew her actual motivation…

'Being your PA for a week isn't so unusual.'

'But checking out animals and bouncy castles is,' he said, his smile crinkling the laugh lines around his eyes and adding to his charm. 'I'm not sure quite what to expect.'

She relaxed, the wine warming her from the inside out while the easy-going camaraderie they shared surrounded her in a comforting cocoon. 'In this business, I'm used to handling anything, so stick with me and you'll be fine.'

'Does that mean you'll protect me from rabid raccoons and scary clowns?'

Crooking her finger at him, she leaned forward. 'I'll let you in on a secret. We don't have raccoons in Melbourne, let alone rabid ones. As for the clowns, they're just make-believe. But, rest assured, if Your Highness is in any danger from cute furry animals or kids' entertainers, I'll protect you.'

He joined in her laughter and she leaned back, the sting of tears taking her completely by surprise.

Tears? What was happening to her? She never cried. Not any more. She'd shed enough to fill the Pacific Ocean when she'd discovered the truth behind Clay's impulsive proposal and later over her mum's death. Tears were wasteful, futile and draining.

She had more important things to worry about these days, like the Towers surviving.

If a glass of wine and some light-hearted conversation made her this maudlin, she'd never make a dating diva. Her impulsive decision to share a drink with him would definitely be her last, if this was how she carried on!

Forcing a hearty laugh, she ignored the real reason behind her sudden self-pity. She liked the warmth, the shared conversation, the time with Dante, and the thought she would soon lose it saddened her more than she expected.

*You don't have to think beyond tomorrow or next week. Just enjoy his company, maybe a dinner here or there, and that's it. Your confidence is low, what better way to build it up than with a guy who looks like Dante paying you compliments?*

Mistaking her sudden downturn in mood, he said, 'Forgive my lame attempts at humour. I'll be fine with the animals, even imaginary raccoons, I promise.'

Natasha drained her glass, and placed it on a coaster on the side table.

'Your humour is fine; it's this marvellous

wine that has me rather tired and drifting off. I'm sorry for being such poor company.'

As if sensing her need for solitude, he placed his half-empty glass on the table and stood, extending a hand to help her up.

'I'm being insensitive. You've worked hard all day in the hotel and then I've made you work even harder with my business. Thank you for sharing the wine and your company, but it is time to say goodnight.'

She accepted his hand, her knees wobbling slightly as she stood, though that had nothing to do with the fine wine and everything to do with the finer prince's welcoming touch.

'Thank you,' she said, matching his formality, her heart sinking at the yawning gap between them. He may try to look the part of a bad-boy, but when he spoke like that he drew her attention to their differences and put her fanciful imagination firmly back in its place. 'I'll see you tomorrow.'

'Until then.'

Their gazes locked, and for one, insane second she thought he would raise her hand to his lips and kiss it. Instead, he gave it a gentle squeeze and released it. Acute disappointment effectively doused the alcohol in her system.

She managed a tremulous smile as they

parted in the foyer, her stomach doing funny flip-flops as she watched him enter the lift.

Crazy.

She was one-hundred-percent crazy for turning what could've been a pleasant evening into a tense mess.

She'd been so busy mulling over Dante's intentions lately, wondering if he was toying with her, if there was more behind needing her help with his family business, that she'd stopped being able to consider the situation rationally.

So, her confidence was at an all-time low. She didn't have to impress the guy, just lighten up a little and enjoy his company. No big deal.

Natasha straightened and headed for her office, silently vowing to loosen up around Dante, starting tomorrow.

'Not a raccoon in sight.'

'Lucky for you,' Natasha said, her gaze riveted to Dante's denim-clad butt as he bent over to pick up a rabbit. So, there was no harm in looking. She could appreciate a fine tail— rabbit, of course!—like the next girl.

'We don't have places like this in Calida. I'm impressed.'

Dante cuddled the white furry rabbit he'd picked up close against his broad chest.

Natasha quickly looked away before she decided to take the rabbit's place.

The guy was gorgeous, rich, genuinely nice and loved animals?

There had to be a catch.

Maybe he hid a pointy tail beneath those faded denims and kept his pitchfork in the closet?

'The animals are pretty cute,' she said, picking up a Dalmatian puppy and laughing as it licked under her chin. 'Make that seriously cute.'

'You said it,' he said, his gaze unerringly locked on her and not on the wriggling puppy in her arms.

Oh boy.

Heat crept into her cheeks as she bent down and placed the puppy next to its siblings, giving it a final pat with reluctance. One of the drawbacks of spending her life growing up in a hotel was the 'no pets' policy. She'd petted other kids' guinea pigs and kittens at school, but it wasn't till recently that she really craved the company and unconditional love of a pet.

Dogs didn't usually turn on their buddies—unlike smarmy fiancés.

Standing up and dusting off her turquoise jacket, she said, 'Okay. I take it the animals are a hit. I'll organise the booking. Day after tomorrow? Eleven a.m.?'

'Sounds good,' Dante said, smiling at her like she'd worked some kind of miracle rather than found suitable entertainment for his nephew's party.

'Okay then.'

But Natasha didn't move. She wanted to, but her feet wouldn't co-operate. Instead, her attention stayed riveted to Dante's hands and the gentle way they stroked the previously quivering rabbit, which had stilled and seemed quite content to burrow into his arms.

She couldn't blame the animal for that. It looked like a mighty comfortable place to be.

Stroke…stroke…soft, rhythmic strokes, with those strong yet elegant hands, a gently lulling motion which she could've watched for ever. She suddenly wished for a pair of long ears and a fluffy tail!

'Bouncy castles next?'

Her gaze snapped up to his, curiosity lighting the blue depths of his eyes, and she mentally slapped herself for being so out of touch with guys that the mere sight of one patting a rabbit had her hypnotised.

'You bet. Meet me at the front desk. We'll finalise the deposit then it's onto something you'll be great at testing out.'

His forehead crinkled in confusion and she

laughed. 'Castles? You being royalty and all? Or has this anonymity for a week gone to your head?'

He chuckled, a forced sound with no genuine amusement in it.

'Do you live in a castle?'

They hadn't talked about his sovereignty much. In fact, they hadn't talked much at all, unless it involved perpetrating his subterfuge, organising his nephew's party or her lack of social skills. What better way to loosen up a little and learn something about the guy in the process?

'Yes. It has been in my family for generations,' he said, placing the rabbit back in its pen and dusting off his hands.

Okay, so he didn't want to elaborate. Maybe if she lightened the mood he'd be more forthcoming.

'Complete with drawbridge, moat and dungeons?'

His mouth twitched. 'No, but it does have a fire-breathing dragon. Its name is Elena.'

'Sounds harmless enough.'

He rolled his eyes. 'You haven't met my mother!'

Natasha laughed, enjoying Dante's reversion to being teasing and funny. She didn't like the serious expression she'd glimpsed earlier, like he shouldered the weight of his country on his shoulders.

'Is your mum that bad?'

'She's been trying to marry me off for years. Looks like my stalling tactics won't work much longer.'

'Oh?'

He grimaced. 'Mother wants to hand over the throne to me as soon as possible. I need a wife for the country to take me seriously, for the people to see me as a genuine monarch and not some playboy prince. She's pushing and, quite frankly, I'm sick of running from the responsibility.'

'That's some responsibility,' she said, her heart sinking that this vibrant, fun-loving guy would be forced into a marriage he didn't want.

Or, if she were completely honest, was she more upset at the thought of Dante married?

Not that it affected her one way or another. He'd be out of her life once his business in Australia was concluded and she'd never hear from him again.

Which is exactly why this whole 'lightening up' thing wasn't such a great idea. It led to all sorts of fantasies, like seeing herself living in a fairy tale castle beside her Prince Charming, just like she'd always imagined as a little girl growing up.

But life wasn't a fantasy. At least, not for her.

She had harsh realities to face up to, and a fair few responsibilities of her own. She could definitely empathise with him there.

'Let's not talk about that now. I'd prefer to concentrate on my time here in Melbourne,' he said, laying a guiding hand in the small of her back and propelling her towards the barn door. 'If my carefree days end when I get back to Calida, I intend to make the most of my stay in your beautiful city.'

'Good idea,' she said.

And it was. It made perfect sense.

Then why the awful feeling that she was just another attraction of Melbourne he intended on having a little fun with before he ascended to the throne?

*Isn't that what you want? To have some fun, flirt, relax with a guy who won't pressure you?*

Of course she wanted that. She'd decided as much last night after her chat with Ella.

Then why the hollow, empty feeling that there was more to life than fun?

For a girl who hadn't had any light-hearted fun in a long time, she shouldn't even be thinking long term. That was what had got her into trouble with Clay in the first place: limited romantic history, falling totally for the first guy to·pay more than two seconds' attention to her, envisaging the whole 'white wedding' thing way too early.

Here was her golden opportunity to ease back into the dating stakes with a little harmless flirtation, and what was she doing? Worrying about whether he was dabbling with her or not.

She really needed to get a life.

'Is something wrong?'

Realising she hadn't moved past the doorway, she shook her head and sent him a confident smile. 'No. Just thinking about how much fun I'm going to have watching you test run the bouncy castles.'

'Is that right?'

His answering smile warmed her from the inside out, like the richest, sweetest hot chocolate.

'That's right. So come on, Your Highness. Let's see what you're made of.'

As they left behind the smells of warm, clean animals and dry hay, Natasha knew that whatever happened she intended on making the most of her limited brush with royalty.

'You call that jumping?'

Dante glared at Natasha, who was the smarter of the two of them, standing with both her feet firmly planted on the ground while he bounced around a huge piece of colourful blown-up plastic like a lunatic.

'If you're so clever, Miss Telford, why don't you show me how it's done?'

He folded his arms, which didn't improve his situation. He wobbled and would've fallen flat on his face if he hadn't stepped wider and braced himself.

'You're on,' she said, clambering up into the giant mock castle, complete with turrets and windows. 'Now, move over and you'll see what jumping's all about.'

However, he didn't move. He just stood there like a star-struck kid and watched a stunning woman bounce around him like a madwoman. A very beautiful madwoman, with her dark, shimmering hair streaming out behind her like a chocolate ripple, her hazel eyes glittering gold in the soft light filtering through the castle windows, and a smile on her face he'd never seen before.

He'd seen her forced smile, her polite smile, her business smile, but he'd never seen her like this. She looked genuinely happy, like she was having a good time, and he was glad.

Make that ecstatic.

He'd been completely honest with her earlier, as much as it had pained him to discuss the situation back home. Time enough to face his responsibilities. For now, he wanted to enjoy himself and, if it so happened to be in the company of a lovely woman like Natasha, all the better for him.

'Come on. Let's see who can jump the highest.' Her grin widened as she placed her thumb on her nose and wiggled her fingers at him. 'Unless His Highness is too chicken, that is?'

With a mock growl, Dante crouched and pushed up with all his strength, propelling himself high into the air. Natasha clapped her hands and laughed loudly. Until he came back down.

With the force of his jump, his landing wasn't so soft, and the rubbery floor moved in a wave beneath his feet, tossing Natasha into the air like a featherweight. She landed in an undignified heap in the far corner of the castle, and Dante was torn between helping to her feet and keeping his distance in case he couldn't let her go once he helped her up.

'Good one. Lucky jump,' she said, leaping to her feet and bouncing towards him like a man walking on the moon.

'Are you all right?'

'Never better.'

He had to agree. Her eyes hadn't lost their sparkle and her cheeks glowed with vitality.

And that mouth… With a jolt, Dante realised he wanted to kiss her. Badly.

When he'd kissed her outside the hotel as part of his pathetic ruse, it had been an impulse. Yes, he'd enjoyed it, and yes he'd been fantasising about more. Hell, he was a red-blooded male, and who wouldn't want the luscious woman before him in their arms?

But this was different.

His gaze strayed to her lips, stayed there, riveted by their fullness, their gloss, their delicious shape.

He wanted her with a ferocity that stunned him, and there weren't too many things in this world that surprised him any more. He'd seen a lot and done a lot in his time.

However, nothing in his past had prepared him for this unfamiliar helpless feeling, wanting something but with no idea how to go about getting it.

Or what he'd do with it if he got it.

'Okay. You asked for it.'

Natasha jumped, breaking his concentration, and in a second he was jumping alongside her as they laughed and jostled and fell about like a couple of kids.

'You like?'

'I most certainly do,' he said, falling in an

undignified heap next to her as they ricocheted off each other and collapsed to the rubber floor.

However, he wasn't talking about the castle, and by the gleam in her incredible eyes she knew it.

He expected her to look away as she'd done repeatedly before when he'd half flirted with her but she surprised him. She rolled onto her side, propped her head on her hand and stared right back.

'You know we're lying where thousands of grubby kids have jumped before?'

'So?'

'We'll probably get kid cooties.'

'Cooties?'

She smiled, a soft upward tilting of her lips that had him aching to reach out and trace their shape.

'You really are a prince, aren't you?'

'Did you doubt it before?'

Her smile widened, her teeth gleaming white in the filtered light. 'You don't exactly look the part.'

'And how do I look?'

'Like the type of guy my mum would've warned me to stay away from.'

'Ouch!'

He clutched his heart in mock pain, wishing

she hadn't lost her smile when she'd mentioned her mother.

For some bizarre reason, lying here with her in the semi-darkness on an old piece of rubber invited questions, confidences, and he didn't want to lose the tentative connection he'd established with her. He thought he'd made a start on building bridges last night when she'd accepted his invitation to have a drink with him, but it hadn't happened and they'd parted on uncomfortably formal terms.

For some reason, he sensed she didn't trust him and, though he liked her honesty, she harboured secrets, bearing an undercurrent of emotion tinged with sadness. Perhaps if he drew her out, got her talking about herself, she'd learn to look at him like he wasn't the ruthless king out to trample on his serfs.

'You haven't mentioned your parents much before,' he said, expecting the shutters to come down, and pleasantly surprised when they didn't.

'My dad's in Perth on business for a month. He'll be back soon.' She paused, sadness flickering across her face like a shadow. 'Mum died a while ago. Heart attack.'

'I'm sorry,' he said, placing a comforting hand on her arm before thinking better of it.

Touching her so soon on the heels of his

earlier impulse wouldn't be a good thing. No telling what he might do in the muted evening light in a mock castle with the most beautiful woman he'd ever seen.

Sadness fell across her face like a dark cloak. 'Thanks. It was tough. We were really close.'

'And there I was complaining about my own mother. You must think I'm heartless.'

And an unfeeling clod for blundering into territory he wished he'd never entered. Inviting confidences was one thing; making her sad after the evening they'd had was downright stupid.

'Everyone has their own demons to battle.'

She softened her words with a tentative smile, but not before he'd glimpsed the darkness in her eyes again, a darkness bordering on fear, the same fleeting expression he'd seen several times as if she had some awful secret weighing her down.

'I think all that jumping around has rattled our brains and made us morbid. How about we have a coffee?'

He wanted to say a meal, but thought better of it. She'd refused his dinner invitation last night; he wouldn't push his luck. He'd made inroads tonight, establishing more of a friendly interaction in how they related, and he didn't want to ruin it.

Besides, he had another favour to ask her and he had a feeling she'd draw the line at this one.

'Sounds great.'

She jumped up and dusted off her butt, sending a sizzle of heat shooting through him. She had a great body, and knew how to accentuate it. Tonight, she wore a soft, turquoise cashmere jacket, a clingy beige top underneath and camel hipsters with matching high-heeled boots. The outfit highlighted her light tan and chocolate-brown hair to perfection, and he'd been staring at her all night.

For a guy who'd socialised with the most beautiful women in the world, from supermodels, actresses and princesses, he'd never been as drawn to anyone as he was to her. Ironic, considering he couldn't do anything about it no matter how much he wanted to. There was a price to pay for his birthright, and at times like this it really hit home.

Sliding to the ground, he held out his arms to help guide her down. She hesitated a fraction and he wondered why. Surely he hadn't scared her off that much?

'Promise I won't drop you,' he said, lifting his arms higher.

'That's not what I'm afraid of,' she muttered under her breath, and as she leaned forward he placed his hands around her waist and gently lifted her to the ground.

If he were prone to theatrics, he could've sworn time stood still as she stood toe to toe with him, her hands braced lightly against his chest while his rested on her trim waist, their gazes locked while tension stretched between them like a taut elastic band.

Her floral fragrance enveloped him, teasing him to do what he'd wanted to do earlier—pull her close and kiss her senseless. To savour her warmth, banish her demons, do whatever it took to assuage the burning need he had for her.

'Thanks,' she said, breaking the loaded silence, snapping him back to reality.

He couldn't do it to her. Natasha was a woman with problems, and he didn't want to add to them by having a quick fling with her before heading home. She didn't deserve that. No matter how much he wanted her.

'At your service.' He released her and did a mock bow, relieved when she laughed. 'If m'lady is tired of playing in her castle, we can retire to the nearest café?'

'Lead the way,' she said, and as she tucked her hand into his proffered elbow he wished it didn't feel so damn right.

# CHAPTER EIGHT

'I'LL take the lot.'

Natasha rolled her eyes at Dante, who looked like a little boy in a toy shop. An apt analogy, considering he was a big boy in a toy shop, and not just any toy shop. The king of toy shops, a toy super-megastore, a place she'd never had reason to visit but couldn't blame him for liking. She'd been pretty smitten herself from the second she'd set foot inside the massive front doors.

'You can't buy everything,' she said, belatedly realising that actually he could. 'I think you should choose between the toddler train-set, the building blocks, the farmhouse or the tunnel and tent.'

He stared at the toys, his brow furrowed as if she'd asked him to make a choice between which heads of government received access to trade talks with Calida.

'The decision is a difficult one. I can't choose.'

Okay, if Dante was behaving like a little boy, she'd use the same reverse psychology on him as she would with any kid.

Shrugging her shoulders, she said, 'Fine. If you want Paolo to be a spoiled rich kid, take the lot. It'll be good for him to know that when he breaks one toy, he'll have a whole heap of others from his uncle to choose from.'

Dante's frown deepened. 'I don't want him to be a spoiled brat.'

He hesitated for only a second before pointing to the train set, a colourful conglomeration of multiple trains made from big stacking blocks, perfect for little hands, wide wooden tracks and enough extra blocks for the odd station or two. It should keep Paolo occupied for the next few months.

'I'll take the train set.'

'Good choice,' she said, hiding her triumphant grin behind a smothered cough when he glanced her way. 'And if that offer for coffee still stands I vote we grab one ASAP. I'm all shopped out.'

And drained, more than she'd ever thought possible. Yeah, she'd had a fun evening, but that was just it—having fun with Dante was exhausting. Trying not to preen under his appreciative stare, trying not to melt in a heap at his feet every time he sent her one of his trademark sexy smiles, had been hard work.

It wasn't fair. The guy shouldn't have so much natural sex appeal.

As for the loaded moment back at the jumping castle, she wished it had never happened. Being held in his arms like that, having him stare at her like he desired her, had almost been too much to bear.

She'd barely stopped herself from swaying forward and kissing him. It had been touch and go. He'd touched her, she hadn't wanted to move, but the longer he'd stared at her, and the longer she'd enjoyed it, the more frightened she'd become.

Having fun with Dante was one thing, falling for him another, and she had no intention of going down a one-way street to heartache again.

'Thanks for your help tonight. I couldn't have done any of this without you.'

He gave her arm a gentle squeeze, a friendly, impersonal touch which meant nothing, yet her skin tingled, her pulse raced and she knew that this fun stuff was dangerous. Very dangerous.

'No problems.'

She wished.

From where she stood, Dante Andretti was one big problem. To her overactive imagination, that was.

'I'll pay for the purchase, get them to deliver and we'll have that long-awaited coffee. Does that suit?'

She nodded, hating the way her heart lurched at his fancy words uttered in that deliciously deep voice.

This fun business was playing havoc with her long-dormant hormones. Once Dante left the country, maybe it would be time to try the odd date or two. If this was how she reacted to a guy simply talking to her, she really needed to get out more.

Then again, she'd never gone in for the whole dating thing anyway. Making the Towers flourish had been her main priority for as long as she could remember, and she loved her job.

But what if she lost it?

What if the one thing that had kept her focussed through losing her mum, discovering Clay's scam and coping with the aftermath of both was taken from her? From her dad?

It would probably kill them both, and she'd be responsible for it.

Yeah, so much for her dating plan.

She'd be better off getting rid of Clay once and for all and trying to save the Towers in the process. Easy—not.

'Everything is organised. Are you ready?'

Dante appeared before her, rubbing his hands together like he'd just successfully conducted state business rather than negotiated a simple toy purchase.

'Uh-huh.'

She smiled, enjoying his enthusiasm, marvelling at how easy it was to be in his company.

No pressure, no expectations, just a laid-back feeling she'd never experienced with a guy before. Her time with Clay had been fraught with tension once the initial star-struck stage had worn off; he'd seemed so polished, she'd always been afraid of making a faux pas. She'd aimed to please; he'd always find fault no matter how small or insignificant.

Yet with Dante she felt more relaxed than she had in ages. Strange, considering her problems hadn't eased. If anything, with every day that passed, the screws on the Towers tightened.

Determined not to ruin the evening they'd had, Natasha banished her morbid thoughts and turned to Dante. 'You hungry? Perhaps we could grab dinner along with that coffee?'

He grinned, his face lighting up. 'I didn't want to push my luck.'

'Push away,' she said.

'Dinner it is.'

They fell into step and made it two doors from the toy shop before finding a quaint little trattoria complete with old wooden tables, red-and-white checked tablecloths and candles stuck into empty Chianti bottles.

'You do like Italian food?'

She managed to keep a straight face at his surprised look.

'Of course. I'm Ital—' He broke off at her laughter and shook his head. 'You are teasing me? Or, as I've heard people here say, "pulling my leg"? My sister has also gained this same strange sense of Australian humour. It confuses me.'

'No worries, mate.'

Natasha's exaggerated ocker drawl seemed to confuse Dante further if the tiny frown on his brow was any indication, so she led the way into the restaurant and chose a table near the front window, determinedly ignoring the cosier romantic options tucked away at the back.

'What's your sister like? You haven't said

much about her.' She slid into the chair Dante held out for her, silently thrilled by his old-fashioned manners. 'Must admit, I'm surprised she's giving you total control over her son's birthday party. And even more surprised you're staying at a hotel for your week of anonymity instead of with her.'

Dante's frown deepened. 'Our relationship is complicated.'

Intrigued, Natasha leaned forward. 'Okay, now you have to tell me all about her.'

'Gina is lovely, but a little self-absorbed. She loves to be spoiled and expects it from everyone around her, including her brother, who's been aware of her games since childhood.'

So that's why he'd been so struck by her barb back at the toy shop about spoiling Paolo.

'She's had my mother twisted around her little finger since birth, but being a female she hasn't had the responsibilities of Calida that I have. Once Gina came of age, no one could hold her. I think Mother was almost relieved to have her meet an Australian cattle baron and get married so quickly.'

Mmm…a rebel princess. Looked like that particular trait ran in the family.

'And she's lived here ever since?'

Dante nodded, an intense, brooding expression darkening his eyes to midnight. She'd never seen him so serious, and she bet there was more to this story than he was letting on.

'Gina is a single mother now. I don't blame her husband for leaving. Not many men could live with someone as pushy and opinionated as her. Hence my choice of hotel. I love my sister, but living with her even for a week after all this time would drive me mad.'

Natasha chuckled, trying to lighten the mood. 'Is she that bad, or do you have a case of sibling rivalry going on? You know—the poor prince gets saddled with all the tough stuff while little sis gets to run wild?'

His look could've frozen Hades.

'I don't blame her for wanting freedom but I do blame her for bringing a helpless child into this world and making him suffer for his mother's mistakes. We all have choices to make, and when thoughtless people make stupid choices that affect their family it's unforgivable.'

Icy tentacles of dread seeped through her veins. What would Dante think of her choices—the stupid choices she'd made, and how they'd adversely affected her family? He'd probably look at her with the scarcely disguised contempt he felt for his sister's decisions and she'd hate that.

She didn't want him to see her as some pathetic loser who'd fallen for a slick charmer determined to get what he wanted right from the start.

In fact, she didn't want him to see her as anything other than the woman he'd looked at with ill-concealed desire a scarce hour ago.

Thankfully, he would never know about her past. And, with a little bit of luck, he'd play a major role in shaping her future. The publicity from his stay at the hotel would be a boon. It had to be.

'If you'd rather not talk about this, I understand. Sorry for bringing it up.'

He waved away her apology. 'Don't be. You were simply curious about my family. I should be the one apologizing to you for airing my family's dirty sheets.'

The corners of her mouth twitched. 'Dirty laundry, you mean?'

He snapped his fingers and finally smiled. 'That's it! My English sometimes lapses.'

'Your English is perfect. In fact, I was surprised you didn't have an Italian accent when we first met, but assumed spending the bulk of your education in the UK took care of that.'

A thoughtful gleam glowed in his eyes. 'You studied up on me?'

'Part of my job is to know about the VIPs who stay at the hotel.'

It sounded plausible. Now, if she could only control the heat seeping into her cheeks, perhaps she could stay seated and not slink under the table in embarrassment.

'Attention to detail. Very important,' he said, his steady gaze flicking over her hair, her face and settling on her lips, sending her blush out of control.

Thankfully, the long overdue appearance of a waiter saved her from answering, and while they made hasty choices from the menu and placed their order she deliberately avoided looking at him.

However, once the menus were gone, the pasta ordered and the wine glasses filled, she had no option but to stare at the man who was slowly but surely driving her crazy.

'You have done a superb job with everything I have asked. I am eternally grateful.'

He raised a glass of Chianti her way, something in his tone alerting her to the fact he wanted to say more but wasn't sure how far to push.

'And?'

He took a sip of wine, placed the glass on the table and smiled. 'And I have one more favour to ask, though after our earlier conversation I won't be surprised if you say no.'

'Try me.'

For a second, his blue eyes flashed danger, desire and a host of other possibilities, and she quickly re-phrased, petrified by the glimpse of 'what if' in those aquamarine depths.

'I can't respond if you don't ask.'

He clasped his hands, placed them on the table and leaned forward. She imagined he would look like this when handing down some princely verdict on an indecipherable problem of the world.

'I would like you to be at Paolo's party. You have made the arrangements seem effortless, and I know having your presence there will ensure that nothing goes wrong.'

Oh no.

No, no, no!

Doing a bit of easy legwork was one thing; fronting up to a pushy princess and fending off a dozen two-year-olds?

No way.

'Please? I know it's a lot to ask, but you're remarkable. You have to know that.'

Remarkable? What did he mean by that?

This was getting more complicated by the minute.

'Please say yes.'

Natasha opened her mouth to say no. Her lips formed the word, her tongue rolled around it, but somehow when a word actually came out it sounded suspiciously like a half-muttered yes.

'Yes?'

Sighing in resignation, she nodded. 'Why not? But let me warn you, your publicity duties next week are going to be hell.'

He laughed, a rich, warm sound that rolled over her like the sun's rays on a perfect summer's day. 'As they say in your country, bring it on.'

'You asked for it,' she said, joining in his laughter, her heart quaking.

This felt too good.

The rich garlic and oregano aromas wafting from the kitchen, the cosy ambience, the muted candlelight all served to highlight the fact she was seated opposite one of the nicest, sexiest men she'd ever met.

And she liked him, genuinely liked him. The kind of like that could quite easily turn into something more if she was prone to craziness.

But thankfully she wasn't that kind of girl.

She'd always been sensible, responsible, dedicated.

Then why the niggling feeling that it was time to take a chance on crazy?

'Who is this woman you are bringing to Paolo's party?'

Gina whirled on Dante, her mop of dark curls swinging across her shoulders in riotous abandon, the same way she'd worn her hair since her teens, the same pouting bottom lip, the same self-indulgent-princess expression on her face.

Dante plucked a stuffed olive off the antipasto platter, popped it in his mouth and chewed slowly. He'd never given in to his sister's bossy ways and he sure wasn't about to start now.

'Well?'

Gina planted one hand on a curvy hip and glared, her dark eyes flashing.

'Natasha Telford is a friend. That's all you need to know.'

And was all he was going to tell her.

The more Gina knew, the more she'd dig and probe and interrogate—and make Natasha's life a living hell at the party. He had no intention of putting her through that. She didn't deserve it after all she'd done for him. In fact, no one deserved to be on the receiving end of Gina on a roll.

Gina pouted for another second before shrugging her shoulders and turning away. 'You have many *friends* around the world. What's another one?'

'Natasha's not like that.'

He jumped in too quickly and Gina quirked an eyebrow his way.

'No? Then what's she like?'

Muttering a soft curse, he said, 'She's a nice young woman, and I don't want you giving her a hard time. Got it?'

'Sure.' Gina's smug grin did little to assuage his concerns. If anything, they intensified.

Maybe he'd been wrong to invite Natasha to the party? It had seemed like a great idea at the time. He wanted to get closer to her, to spend as much time as he could with her, and she'd been a real trouper in going along with everything he'd asked of her.

He'd hoped that in spending time with his family she'd see another side to him, a side that wasn't caught up in his heritage and who he was and where he'd have to be in a few weeks' time: back in Calida, in the job he'd been born to, probably engaged to a woman he didn't love.

Somehow, having Natasha see him in a good light had become important to him. He liked her, beyond her beauty and sassy mouth, and a small part of him wanted more. A lot more. But what could that be?

He didn't want to indulge in a tawdry fling with her; she was too special for that.

He didn't have time to explore anything deeper.

The way he saw it, he didn't have many options and, for a smart guy used to making economic decisions for a country and running world-affairs meetings, he didn't like the strange fog pervading his brain when it came to Natasha.

He needed clarity of thought, some idea of what to do about his growing attraction to a woman who sparked him like no other ever had. But he couldn't think beyond how great it felt to spend time with her, and how her caramel eyes glowed with vitality.

'Uh-oh.'

'What?'

Gina waggled a finger at him. 'You've got a funny look on your face, big brother.'

'Probably indigestion from that awful gnocchi you fed me earlier.'

'More like an awful case of wanting to have your cake and eat it too.'

He should've ignored Gina, but Paolo hadn't returned with the nanny yet and he had no option but to face the firing squad. Besides, he did love his sister no matter how painful she could be and they rarely got to see each other these days.

'Okay, I'll bite. What's that supposed to mean?'

'We both know Mother will have you betrothed as soon as you step off the plane in Calida. She won't hand over the crown without you being engaged, so this thing with your *friend* Natasha is your way of having what you want before getting what you don't.'

Gina smiled, but Dante sensed a tinge of sadness behind it rather than smug satisfaction or her usual gloating. 'I don't envy you, that's for sure. Must be tough having your life mapped out.'

*You don't know the half of it,* Dante thought.

'It's my duty.'

'But is it what you want?'

Dante cast a quizzical look Gina's way. He'd never seen her like this: serious, interested in him rather than the latest fashion trend.

'It's irrelevant what I want.'

He'd learned that from an early age.

When the village kids had skipped down to the water's edge and jump off the cliffs into the crystal clear azure sea, he'd been flanked by surly bodyguards warning him of the dangers.

When his few teenage friends had wanted to ride beat-up old scooters around the island, he'd had to stay behind to entertain the neighbouring island's king's son.

And when he finally reached a legal age when he could've done anything he wanted like other guys his age, he'd been busy taking diplomacy lessons and learning to speak eight languages.

No, it didn't matter what he wanted. It never had.

To his surprise, Gina crossed the short space separating them and gave him a quick hug. 'You're one of the good guys. And, believe it or not, I'm on your side.'

'Thanks,' he said, thankful he'd made this trip to Australia. Gina was doing okay, Paolo was adorable and he'd seal a few trade deals next week.

As for Natasha, he still had no idea where they went from here.

And it was killing him.

# CHAPTER NINE

'LET me get this straight. He's taking you to a kid's party?'

Ella shook her head, tore the top off a sugar sachet and tipped the contents into her black coffee. 'For a prince, the guy has no idea how to impress a woman.'

'He's not trying to impress me,' Natasha said, sipping her mocha-cappuccino and sighing with pleasure.

He didn't have to. Dante already impressed her just by being him.

Last night had sealed it.

Not only was he one of the sexiest men to walk the planet, he didn't seem to have many faults from where she stood. He was polite, cultured, approachable and, oh... Did she mention sexy?

Then he had to go and pull out the big guns, showing her his soft side for animals and toys. It wasn't fair. If she hadn't liked him before, she would've fallen at his feet the minute he'd picked up that adorable rabbit and cuddled it close.

'I think it's sweet he's taking me to his nephew's party,' she said, spooning the last of a chocolate-cream cannoli into her mouth and smiling like she'd just gone to heaven. She'd tasted every sweet in Luigi's range, and every calorie-laden morsel was to die for.

Ella's eyes narrowed. 'Whoa! Hold on a sec. You didn't tell me it was his nephew's party! That puts an entirely different slant on proceedings.'

'You make it sound like a law case,' Natasha said, not minding her friend's interrogation one bit.

It was a gorgeous Melbourne day, the type of crisp spring day with a hint of chill in the air but the glorious sun to warm you. Throw in the fact she'd just finished her third-to-last shift as stand-in concierge, organised another payment to Clay, and the end of the week was looming bringing her one step closer to saving the Towers with Dante's help, and life couldn't be better.

Well, it could be, if the Towers was safe and Dante wasn't a prince destined to ride off into the sunset in the not too distance future but, hey, no use wishing for the impossible.

She'd learned that a long time ago.

'What's your take on the party?' Natasha lay down her fork and pushed away her plate, patting her stomach with a groan.

'Simple,' Ella said, snapping her fingers like a magician conjuring up doves out of a hat. 'He wants to introduce you to the family. Serious stuff.'

Natasha rolled her eyes. 'It's only his sister. And he's only asking me along to make sure nothing goes wrong with the animals or the bouncy castle.'

'He can pay any old body to do that,' Ella said, stirring her coffee before taking a sip. 'Want to know what I think?'

'I'm sure you'll tell me anyway.'

'He wants to get the royal stamp of approval. You know, like having you vetted before taking any big steps.'

'You're out of your mind,' Natasha muttered, hating the tiny, irrational surge of hope deep in her soul that her friend could be right.

She'd never been any good at playing the 'what if' game, but since she'd met Dante she'd found herself doing it all the time.

What if the attraction between them meant something?

What if it grew into something more?

What if fairy tales did come true and she

finally got the happily ever after she'd only ever dreamed about?

But 'what ifs' could be painful. They led to silly dreams and big let-downs. If anyone should know, she should. The way she looked at it, the only big steps Dante would be taking around her involved him heading in the direction of the airport and all the way back to Calida.

Ella shrugged. 'Hey, it's just my opinion.'

'And I don't need that sort of pressure. I'm just enjoying spending time with the guy, remember?'

'Uh-huh. Besides, you don't need anyone's stamp of approval. You're fine just the way you are.'

'Thanks for the vote of confidence.' Natasha grinned at Ella's quick backtrack. 'Being with Dante is fun, and it's been a long time since I've had any. So lighten up, will you?'

Looking suitably chastised for all of two seconds, Ella took a few gulps of coffee before chirping up again. 'Big steps. You'll see.'

Ella ducked under a barrage of scrunched up serviettes and empty sugar sachets while Natasha decided she needed to improve her aim.

*Big steps...big steps...*

Uh-uh—she wouldn't go there.

She wouldn't even contemplate what it could mean if Ella was right.

For now, she was safer sticking with her original theory. Big steps only led to big trampling, and she had no intention of getting caught underfoot of any guy ever again.

'So this is why you wanted the gift delivered?'

Natasha cast a dubious look over the gleaming Harley waiting at the kerb, its chrome shining and in perfect contrast to the highly polished black paint.

Dante smiled and held out a helmet to her. 'It's the only way to travel,' he said, while she silently begged to differ. 'Ever been on a bike before?'

She shook her head, not quite convinced she ever would. Though the bike was big, it still appeared too flimsy lined up against the cars, trucks and SUVs on Melbourne's busy roads.

'It's easy. Just hold on tight and you'll be fine.'

Okay, so he'd convinced her.

She might be afraid of big mechanical things she couldn't control, but the thought of being plastered against Dante's back with her arms wrapped tight around his waist held a certain appeal.

Besides, what had happened to her 'let's just have fun for now' motto?

'Okay.'

She slipped the helmet over her head, fiddling with the chin strap for a second before Dante reached over and cinched it. Her breath hitched as his fingers brushed the skin under her chin, the barest and lightest of touches, enough to send heat ripping through her body.

Her eyes closed involuntarily as she savoured the unusual sensation, the purely visceral reaction of a strong, uncontrollable attraction. She'd never experienced anything like it and it was heady stuff.

'You sure you're going to be okay? We can always take a cab.'

Natasha opened her eyes, her gaze connecting with Dante's concerned one.

'I'll be fine. I haven't had much to eat today, just felt a bit woozy for a second.'

She tried not to cringe at how pathetic she sounded but, thankfully, he bought it.

'Gina has catered enough food to feed the entire population of Calida, so we'll get you something when we arrive. Is that soon enough, or would you prefer a quick snack before we go?'

'I'm fine, really,' she said, feeling increasingly guilty and finding it difficult not to laugh.

She'd told him she was hungry. Unfortunately, it wasn't for food, and she wondered what he'd think if he knew he was the tastiest dish on her menu right now.

'Sure?'

She nodded and clambered on before she changed her mind. 'Sure.'

Dante didn't move, grinning at her like a loon. She guessed the sight of her perched on the back of a bike didn't look as cool as she hoped. Thankfully, she'd worn black hipsters and a matching polo but perhaps the buckled up salmon-pink trench coat was a bit much?

Then again, it wasn't her fault. She'd been expecting a civilised mode of transport, not to play out some biker chick role.

'You going to ride this thing, or just look at it?'

Ignoring her brisk tone, his smile broadened as he climbed aboard, and that's when the fun really started.

Before starting the engine, Dante ensured her arms were clasped firmly around his waist, and as she dug her fingers into the buttery soft leather of his black jacket a thrill of pure anticipation shot through her.

Now, this was exciting!

As he revved the engine and carefully pulled into traffic, Natasha closed her eyes and sent a silent prayer heavenward.

*Please let me be safe…*

The bike shot forward, turned several corners and hit the beach road curving along Port Phillip Bay. Adrenalin coursed through her body and she'd never felt better but she continued her prayer.

*Let me be safe from falling for a guy like Dante. Please.*

Sadly, as the short ride between the hotel and his sister's beachside mansion ended, she had a sinking feeling it was too late.

'Do I have helmet hair?'

Dante took the helmet Natasha held out to him and stared at her like she'd just spoken Martian.

'Helmet hair?'

She chuckled. He was adorably, royally stuffy at times and didn't have a clue.

'Is my hair messy from wearing the helmet?'

Realisation made his blue eyes sparkle, and before she could move he reached out and tucked a strand of hair behind her ear.

'Your hair looks fine.'

His fingers brushed her earlobe as he withdrew his hand, sending a delicious shiver through her body.

Maybe it was the last ten minutes being plastered against his body, maybe it was the heat radiating off his body and warming her better than the sun's rays, but whatever it was her body seemed super-sensitised to him.

For goodness' sake, all he'd done was touch her hair and brush her ear and her body was in orbit. Time to douse her fever with a little reality check; an hour in the company of twenty toddlers and his sister should do the trick.

'You look beautiful,' he said, sending her one of his sexy trademark smiles that made her *feel* beautiful. 'Now, if you're ready, time to face the firing squad.'

'Firing squad?'

She didn't have time to ask anything else as a woman wearing a blinding-white designer suit and a monstrous matching wide-brimmed hat strode up to them.

'You must be Natasha.'

'That's right.'

Natasha took the proffered hand of the stunning woman and smiled.

'I'm Gina. Welcome.'

Though Gina's smile seemed genuine enough, Natasha saw the cool, calculating gleam in her eyes and suddenly she wished she hadn't come.

This was ludicrous. Helping Dante and spending a casual evening over dinner was one thing, getting sized up by his family another.

'Now that you two lovely ladies have met, shall we join the party in the rear garden? I can hear the kids squealing from here.'

Dante's light touch in the small of her back soothed Natasha's slightly frayed nerves and she straightened, determined to enjoy the party.

Gina extended an arm towards her endless cobbled driveway. 'Please come through.'

Her voice sounded formal and somewhat stilted, and Natasha marvelled at the difference between brother and sister. Where Dante's eyes were piercing blue, Gina's were almost coal black. While Dante spoke with a casual lilt, Gina's upper class accent screamed status, wealth and power.

'Paolo hasn't stopped asking for you since the castle and animals arrived an hour ago. He's very impressed. And so am I.'

Gina's praise almost sounded begrudging, and Natasha pondered the strange undercurrent which passed between brother and sister when Dante glared at her.

'I couldn't have done it without Natasha,' he said, his smile warming her from the inside out.

'Mmm.'

Gina's guarded response and sideways stare almost sent Natasha scuttling back to the motorbike, but at that second a small boy ran around the corner of the sandstone mansion, screamed and lunged towards Dante.

'Hey, Paolo, my little man. Happy birthday,' Dante said, squatting down to hug the little boy close before picking him up and swinging him high in the air, eliciting more ear-splitting shrieks.

Natasha's breath caught in her throat as she watched Dante and Paolo pull apart, their foreheads touching as they rubbed noses in an Eskimo kiss.

The emotion on their faces, the joy of a special shared moment, made her heart clench.

She wanted that.

She wanted a special connection, the type of heart-wrenching elation that came with being with the right person, with sharing a family with that person.

And right then, right there, standing in the waning afternoon sunlight on a clear Melbourne day, it hit her.

She wanted that special connection with Dante.

A tremor shuddered through her body and she stiffened, reluctant to acknowledge the startling revelation, determined to ignore it.

It must've been the excitement of that darn motorbike ride. The stupid speed machine had rattled her brain. But the longer she tried to deny it, the more her gaze was drawn to the cosy picture of uncle and nephew cuddling, and how much Dante affected her.

'Dante's smitten with my son.'

Natasha managed a polite smile for Gina and nodded. 'He sure is. Not that I blame him. Your son's adorable.'

'Spoken like a woman who doesn't have children.' Gina's cynical laugh raised the hairs on the back of Natasha's neck, and she racked her brain for something to say.

'You have a lovely home. Do you enjoy living in Melbourne?'

'Melbourne is convenient. We're settled here now, and it's far enough away from Calida to keep me sane.'

The bitterness in Gina's voice surprised Natasha and before she could say anything else, or make frantic eye signals in Dante's direction for him to save her from his scary sister, Gina stepped closer and dropped her tone to barely whisper pitch.

'Dante's not like me, though. He's a born and bred Calidian. It's his destiny.'

'I'm sure it is,' Natasha said, wishing she'd opted for a quiet afternoon in her room rather than this.

'You know this thing with you can't be serious, don't you? When he returns, he'll be taking a bride and ascending to the throne, so don't grow too attached. My brother has a duty to our homeland and won't give that up even for…what you can offer. After the trouble you've gone through for my son's party, I feel it only fair I warn you.'

Icy dread trickled through Natasha's veins. Nothing Gina said surprised her. She'd known Dante had responsibilities back home; he'd said as much. As for what she could offer, it didn't take a genius to figure out what the woman was implying.

But it still hurt.

The cold, harsh reality that Dante could only be toying with her, hoping for a final fling before settling down, hurt. A lot.

Fixing a brittle smile in place, she nodded at Gina. 'Thanks for your concern, but Dante and I are just friends.'

With that, Natasha forced her feet to move and walked over to Dante and Paolo, where the little curly-haired cherub took one look at her and ducked his head into the crook of his uncle's shoulder.

'Paolo, meet my friend Natasha. She helped me bring the animals and bouncy castle here. And, later, you'll see what she helped me choose for your present. Say hello.'

Dante winked at her and tickled Paolo, who lifted his head and peeked at her with wonder in his dark eyes.

'Tasha? My birfday?'

Natasha's heart melted as she stepped forward and gently ruffled the little boy's hair. 'Yes, sweetheart, happy birthday. Are you having fun?'

Paolo nodded, a hint of a grin tugging at his mouth. 'Fun, fun!'

'Can I see the animals? Will you show me?'

'Yeah!'

Paolo wriggled in Dante's arms, and they laughed as he placed the strapping boy down on his feet, where he promptly shot off towards the back yard, stopping for a brief second to see if they were following.

'You coming, Gina?' Dante called over his shoulder while Natasha wondered if she could bolt after Paolo and thus escape spending any more time with Gina.

'I've got some things to take care of inside. You go ahead.'

Natasha's sigh of relief must've been audible as Dante fell into step beside her. 'Did Gina say something to upset you?'

'No, why?'

The little white lie popped out easily. She had

no intention of letting him know how rattled she was, first by the stunning realisation of how much he meant to her, closely followed by how little she must mean to him.

'My sister has a habit of saying the wrong things, and you had a strange look on your face when you walked up to Paolo.'

'Gina didn't tell me anything I didn't already know,' she said, managing to keep the sadness out of her voice with difficulty.

She'd never been one for crying. Sure, she'd cried buckets when her mum had died, and even when Clay had shown his true colours, but she'd grown stronger since then. She'd had to.

Then why the sudden, dreadful urge to sink onto the nearest stone bench in the shade of a huge maple and bawl her eyes out?

'What did she say?'

Dante laid a hand on her arm but she didn't stop. Instead, she shrugged him off and fixed the best smile she could muster in place.

'Nothing important. Now, we've got a party to go to.'

Even if celebrating was the last thing she wanted to do.

# CHAPTER TEN

NATASHA would've liked nothing better than to go to her room, sink into a warm bath and listen to a relaxation CD. If playing the happy party person had shredded her nerves, riding up close and personal with Dante on the way home had undone her completely.

However, the minute she caught sight of Clay waiting for her in the Lobby Bar, she knew her wish for solitude would have to wait.

She had business to conduct and, in the mood she was in, Lord help her ex if he put a foot wrong.

'Thanks for accompanying me to Paolo's party.'

If Dante had bowed to go along with his formal little speech she wouldn't have been surprised. Somehow, he'd picked up on her reticent vibes and was reacting accordingly.

Good. Only two more days, and at the end of

the week his visit here would become public knowledge and, soon after, he could return to his *responsibilities*. None the wiser to the fool she'd almost made of herself.

'No problems. Thanks for asking me.'

He didn't move, his steady gaze searching her face, as if looking for clues to her sudden turnaround in behaviour. Well, he could keep looking. She'd mastered the art of the poker face a long time ago, around the first time Clay had demanded payment, and she'd been forced to go along with it for the sake of her family.

'Would you like a nightcap? A cocoa, perhaps?'

'No,' she blurted quickly, realising how rude it sounded a second too late. 'Thanks, but I'd rather not. Good night, Dante.'

She couldn't bear to see the bewildered, almost hurt look in his eyes so she turned away quickly and walked towards the front office.

'Good night, Tasha,' he said, his low voice not affecting her as much as his use of the pet name Paolo had given her.

Something about the way he said it—soft, personal, intimate, as if he'd never called her anything else—made tears spring to her eyes, and she blinked rapidly to dispel them.

She couldn't show weakness in front of Clay.

He thrived on that sort of thing, something she'd learned far too late.

Natasha ducked into the front office, waited till Dante took the express lift, before stepping out and crossing the marble foyer to the Lobby Bar. Taking a deep breath, she patted her back pocket, felt the reassuring rustle of paper and headed for the man who had torn her world apart and that of her family.

'You're late,' Clay said, not looking up from his double Scotch on the rocks.

'And you're only welcome here because you're a paying customer.'

She noted the slight flush beneath his collar, deriving petty satisfaction from her barb. It was stupid, and she shouldn't stoop to his level, but he brought out the worst in her these days and, in her current frame of mind, he'd be lucky if she let him walk out of here alive.

Draining his drink in one, long gulp, he swivelled on the bar stool to stare at her with cold avarice in his emotionless eyes. 'You have something for me?'

Meeting his stare, she reached into her back pocket and handed him the folded piece of paper. 'Here.'

She expected him to grab the cheque, scan it like he usually did, slip it into his pocket and give her one of his signature sleazy smiles before strutting out the door. They'd been through this scenario three times previously and, thankfully, there would only be one more.

One more month and she'd be free, her family would be free.

If they didn't lose the Towers in the meantime.

However, this time Clay surprised her. Rather than taking the cheque, he captured her hand and, taking advantage of her shock, used his superior strength to pull her close.

'So, how are things with lover boy? If it doesn't work out, you know I'm more than man enough for you.'

Natasha almost retched as his Scotch-laden breath hit her in the face, but rather than struggle—he would've liked it too much—she went slack against him.

'You're not a man, you're a sub-human with the intelligence of a gnat, with the rest of you in proportion too,' she said, lingering long enough to insult him before pushing off his chest so hard he would've fallen backwards if the bar hadn't propped him up.

'And one more thing. If you ever touch me again, you won't get another cent out of me. I don't care how many threats you throw my way, and I'll let the world know exactly what you are.'

She ignored his string of muttered expletives—she'd heard them all before when she'd exposed him for the creep he was first time around—and walked out the door, head high.

Her heart thumped, her head ached and she wanted to hide away for a week. Instead, she didn't look left or right. She couldn't. She needed the sanctity of her room in the next few minutes before she fell apart.

There was only so much she could take and, after the day she'd had, she'd well and truly reached her limit.

Dante slammed into his room, headed for the mini bar, screwed the top off a sparkling mineral water in record time and drank deeply. He needed to erase the bitter taste in his mouth at what he'd just seen, even if he knew nothing could erase the awful image.

Gripping the half-empty bottle in his fist, he was surprised he didn't crush the glass to sand.

The woman he'd come to like, to respect, and to want more with every passing minute, had been too tired to have a nightcap with him. However, she hadn't been too tired to cosy up to her ex.

He dashed a hand across his eyes, knowing it would do little to erase the memory of the two of them: the creep holding her hand against his chest, her body up close and personal with his, their faces inches apart.

Anger burned deep in his gut. Not at Natasha, who he'd sensed had secrets and wasn't over her ex from the one time he'd seen them together, but at himself for being such a fool.

For letting his guard down, for letting a woman affect him as much as Natasha did. Worst of all, for letting himself believe in the possibility that he didn't have to control everything, that some things were bigger than responsibilities and arranged marriages and duty.

He drained the rest of his drink, threw the bottle in the bin and sank down into a comfy armchair, staring out at the glittering Melbourne skyline.

The city had enchanted him.

*Not as much as Natasha.*

Cursing his inner voice, he allowed his anger to fester, knowing it would be the only emotion to keep him detached enough to not barge back down to the bar and wrench her from her ex's arms.

However, the longer he nursed his anger, the more it grew and morphed into something nastier, swerving direction away from him and pointing straight at the woman who had got to him.

He could've sworn she'd returned his interest: the sparkle he'd glimpsed over dinner, the almost-kiss in the bouncy castle, her tiny, satisfied sigh when she'd first wrapped her arms around him on the bike earlier today.

She'd probably thought he hadn't heard it, but he had and it had shot straight to his heart. That's why he'd asked her for a nightcap, to perhaps explore their mutual attraction, maybe see where things could lead given half a chance.

The crazy thing was, when he was with her he forgot about Calida and his impending duty. In fact, he forgot everything but the way she looked, the way she smelled and how incredible she made him feel. Being with her was a heady rush and he wanted more. Hell, he wanted it all.

He couldn't escape the responsibilities of his birth, but what if he had a woman like Natasha by his side rather than a bride hand-picked by his mother?

The thought had insinuated its way into his head on the way home tonight and he'd wanted time to ponder it, develop it and, most of all, see if the woman in question had the slightest interest in being more for him than a PA or a friend.

Well, he certainly had his answer.

Yes, he'd definitely been a fool.

His mother was right. When the heart ruled the head, it could only end in disaster.

And, like an awful train wreck, he knew he'd have a hard time turning away from Natasha and the havoc she'd wrought.

The throb behind Natasha's eyes intensified, and her fingers shook as she stabbed at the calculator buttons one more time, hoping that by some miracle the numbers would change the more times she entered them.

They didn't.

She'd tried every permutation, every combination, shaving a profit margin here, skimping on a goods purchase there, but the answer was still the same.

She didn't have the money she needed for Clay's last payment.

And she needed the money. Now.

After what she'd just endured downstairs, she couldn't wait another day let alone another month to get rid of him once and for all.

It had taken every ounce of self-control she possessed not to punch him when he'd groped her in the bar. It would've felt so good, but then what sort of example would that set for her staff? Not to mention the stray paying customer that could've strolled in.

Besides, she had more class than that. In fact, for a guy who'd attended the best private schools, and was hung up on appearances and his standing in Melbourne society, Clay had the class of a slug.

Pushing the uncooperative calculator away, she sat back in her chair and rubbed her temples, knowing being free of Clay would soothe her better than any massage or paracetamol.

But how?

Having Dante help with publicity would raise the hotel's profile and bring in much-needed money over the next month, but she needed that money now.

Thoughts swirled around her head: banks, lending societies, business associates, contacts. Around and around, the same avenues she'd exhausted when all this had started, when she'd been foolish enough to agree to Clay's demands in the first place.

But, then, what option had she back then?

Lose the family business at the hands of a bitter and twisted man who had only wanted one thing from their relationship? And it sure hadn't been her!

No way.

She'd got her family into this mess with Clay,

she'd get them out of it. Though it had to be now. She couldn't have him threatening her or the Towers any longer. Tonight had been the final time he'd laud anything over her, or touch her for that matter.

There had to be a way out…something she hadn't thought of…

The harder she concentrated, the more her head ached, but in the midst of random thoughts and wishful thinking a glimmer of an idea took shape.

No, she couldn't.

Sure, she'd established a friendship with Dante, but that didn't mean she could take advantage of his position or status. Besides, she'd always fought her own battles.

Having a prince slay the dragon might hold a certain appeal but she couldn't involve him. She had her pride, and having a virtual stranger witness her folly—a stranger she'd been stupid enough to fall for despite all her self-talk—would be tantamount to running down Bourke Street buck naked.

And hadn't she embarrassed herself enough?

Falling for a prince might be stupid, but harbouring dreams that he felt the same way went way beyond that. Try moronic, self-defeating and crazy.

Gina had done her a favour in setting the record straight and, no matter how much she'd like to pretend otherwise, Dante had been toying with her.

A line from an old Eddie Murphy comedy sprung to mind, something about a prince travelling to the opposite side of the world to sow his royal oats, and unfortunately it looked like Dante had been doing the same.

She should be mortified. In fact, she should be downright affronted at the thought. But she wasn't, and a small part of her knew why.

Something wasn't right.

The scenario Gina had painted might have fitted a lesser man but Dante didn't seem the type. If the guy wanted a fling, why hadn't he pushed her? Hassled her? Flirted outrageously with her, sweet-talked her, tried to sweep her off her feet?

Dante hadn't done any of those things. Sure, he'd flattered her, flirted a little, but his behaviour had been irreproachable.

Surely a guy with less than a fortnight in a foreign country would go for it? Would pull out all stops to get a girl into bed if that was his intention?

Uh-uh, something definitely didn't sit right.

Either Gina was wrong—which begged the

question, why would she lie?—or Dante was playing another type of game.

And, if so, what was it?

# CHAPTER ELEVEN

NATASHA didn't believe in coincidences.

So when she walked into Trevi's, and spotted Dante at a quiet table in the back corner, she wondered if sneaky Ella had played a trick on her.

Not in the mood to face His Royal Sexiness, or ponder the question of his oats, she made for the long, polished teak counter, head down, determined to grab a mocha-cappuccino to go.

'*Ciao*, Natasha! Why is my favourite girl in such a hurry today? You no want to sit?'

Natasha fought a blush as Luigi's bass voice boomed across the café and Dante's head snapped up from the newspaper he'd been buried in.

'Actually, I have lots to do today—'

'Nonsense! You know that nice young man, *si*? The one pushing a chair out for you?'

Luigi pointed straight at Dante and she had

to agree it did appear as if Dante was inviting her to sit down. 'Now, you go and chat while I bring your coffee. And tiramisu?'

Natasha shook her head, the thought of forcing a morsel of food down her throat making her nauseous. She hadn't been able to eat a thing this morning, her mind in a muddle from last night.

Her main problem should be Clay and clearing her debt, but somehow Gina's words kept popping into her head and she'd find herself pondering Dante's motivations, her own, and the complete mess she'd made of her life without trying.

'Just the coffee, thanks, Luigi. And I will take it over there.'

Luigi beamed and she headed to Dante's table, basking in the appreciative once-over he gave her favourite summer dress, annoyed that she cared, and surprised when he blanked his gaze as she drew nearer.

'You don't mind if I join you?'

'Please sit.'

He stood and pulled out her chair further, and as she slid into it she couldn't help but inhale, savouring his citrus scent mingling with the rich aroma of coffee beans and vanilla in the air.

She would miss this. Miss him. His scent, his smile, his company, the works.

She would miss it all when he left and, no matter how hard she tried to sugar-coat it, she knew it would leave her more devastated than she'd thought possible.

'Is something wrong?'

She searched his face, looking for the telltale crinkle of laugh lines around his eyes, the ever-present sparkle in their clear blue depths, the cheeky smile quick to appear at the slightest provocation.

Nothing.

If he'd effectively blanked his stare when she'd reached the table, he'd done a similar job on his face.

Expressionless, devoid of emotion, he stared at her with a forced, polite interest.

'I am leaving today,' he said, his tone dead.

A shiver of apprehension shot through her as she concentrated on his lips, sure she'd just heard him form some words about leaving.

'Leaving?'

Her voice came out a tiny squeak and she cleared her throat, hating the desperation she heard in the one word she'd uttered.

'Yes. I've done what I set out to do.'

'Oh.'

Her mind refused to compute what he'd just said. Sure, he'd taken care of family business as he'd said at the start of the week, but what about the rest? What happened to his official duties?

Suddenly, it hit her like a bolt of electricity, leaving her shocked and breathless and in need of resuscitation. If he didn't stick around for official business, where did that leave her? Or, more precisely, the hotel's publicity she'd been depending on?

'What about our agreement? You said you'd help with the hotel publicity. I've upheld my end of the bargain, what about yours?'

Not a flicker of expression crossed his face. It was like talking to an automaton, and she had an impulse to jump up and down, wave her arms in front of his face and yell, do anything to elicit some emotion, some recognition that she was the woman he'd spent the last week with, chatting, making her laugh, making her feel special.

'You will be suitably compensated,' he said, his cold, flat tone matching the cold, lifeless aquamarine depths she'd seen glitter with fire. 'This should cover it.'

He reached into his pocket and slid a folded piece of paper across the table, his long, elegant fingers lingering over it while she stared at it in disbelief.

He was paying her off.

The small, folded bit of paper had to be a cheque, but she wouldn't give him the satisfaction of looking at it.

'It's that easy for you, isn't it?'

She swallowed, hating the way her voice shook, wishing her heart didn't ache at the thought of him walking out of this café without a backward glance.

She could've fooled herself and attributed the vice-like pain squeezing her heart to the thought of losing the hotel's one-way ticket out of trouble. But she was through lying to herself. What was the point?

She'd suffered through the indignity of Clay's demands and she'd battled on, but losing Dante sent an arrow of pain shooting through the organ she'd learned to protect more than life itself.

Fool.

The cap fit; she'd be the first to admit it. What she hated to acknowledge was, no matter how much self-talk she'd indulged in, she'd still gone ahead and fallen for the wrong guy. Again.

'Easy? You mean my leaving?'

Dante frowned as if he hadn't understood her question.

'Of course. What else could I mean?'

*Easy for you to walk away without a backward glance?*

*Easy for you to flirt a little to get your own way?*

*Easy for you to make someone like me fall for someone like you?*

At least her sarcastic response elicited a reaction out of him, if she could call the slight compressing of his lips a reaction.

Those same lips she'd experienced crushing hers in an all too brief, fake encounter. And, as stupid as she felt at that moment for falling for him, a small part of her couldn't help but wonder what it would've been like to have those lips caress her with serious passion, with intent.

'I thank you for your assistance this week. It has been invaluable, but it is time for me to move on.'

If he'd executed a snappy royal bow to go along with his polite nod and stilted speech, she wouldn't have been surprised.

As for 'it' and not 'you' being invaluable, she could quite easily tip a sachet of arsenic in place of sugar into his coffee for that little gem.

'Guess I shouldn't be surprised at the turn-around.'

'I beg your pardon?'

She could've held her tongue and let him walk away. But, then, since when had she let a guy get away with anything?

She'd called Clay's bluff and, though she'd had to eat humble pie for the sake of her family, Dante couldn't do a thing to hurt her that Clay hadn't already done.

She leaned forward, fixing him with a glare, trying to soothe her bruised ego without losing control of her fragile temper.

'Your turnaround. The whole about-face. You were the laid back, rebel prince one minute, schmoozing up to a pleb to get what you wanted done, and now that's finished you're reverting to type. Using money or power or whatever you have to get the job done. Nice.'

She should've stopped there. In fact, his frigid stare would probably have made the sassiest big mouth shut up, but unfortunately she was on a roll.

She needed to do this, to have her say.

She needed closure, and she knew without a doubt that, by the time she'd finished here, the Dante and Natasha interlude would be well and truly over.

'Are you quite finished?'

'Actually, no. Bear with me for a sec while I tell you a story and then you can walk away.'

She didn't expect him to stay. In fact, she expected him to push his chair back and stroll out of the café and out of her life without a care.

Instead, he sat back, his glacial expression not warming. Then again, after what she'd just said to him, he would've been within his rights to ignore her completely.

'I've met many people in my line of work over the years. Rock stars, film stars, VIPs, families, businessmen, people from every walk of life. Working as a concierge this last week, I've had a bunch of interesting requests, from a guy requesting three hundred and sixty five red roses to be delivered by porters for his wedding anniversary, a media mogul requesting I buy a Porsche for his girlfriend and insisting it had a fuchsia ribbon around it, and a guy who asked me to organise a gondola ride down the Yarra for his girlfriend and a footpath artist to write "will you marry me?" surrounded by love hearts for when they docked.'

She'd actually been a little green at that one. Why couldn't she find a guy who'd go all out to make her feel that special?

Thankfully, Dante hadn't bolted at her long-winded speech and she continued before he did. 'All unique requests, things I managed to deliver without batting an eyelid, and then in walks this rebel prince. Nothing what I expected, mind you. In fact, the antithesis of every preconceived royal idea I had in my head. Of course, he had an unusual request, to preserve his anonymity for a week. Being the good little concierge, I agreed, but you know the part I don't get?'

She'd sparked his interest, glimpsing a flicker of fire in those incredible eyes.

'What's that?'

'The part where the prince masquerading as a pauper went a step further and established a friendship with me. He was fun to be with and he made me feel like I was a part of his life, even for a brief moment.'

*He made me fall for him, to feel things I've never felt before.*

*He made me trust again.*

*He made me wish for a future, no matter how far-fetched or unobtainable.*

*He made me want the fairy tale happy ending.*

Blinking back the sudden sting of tears, she said, 'Then he goes cold on me. Says he's leaving. Just like that. If you ask me, that's stranger than any of those other things I've had to deal with all week.'

Natasha sighed and leaned back, all out of puff. What had started out as an accusatory monologue had petered out to a pathetic cry for answers.

She scanned his face, knowing every plane and angle as if she'd studied it her entire life. She saw the slight widening of his eyes, the tense jaw, and the flash of something akin to anguish cross his face.

That couldn't be right. What did she expect, that he felt pain at walking away after the meaningless week they'd shared?

As if.

'I don't owe you any explanations,' he said, his stony expression unchanging, sending any faint hope she might get closure plummeting.

'No, I guess you don't.'

She glanced away, shame flooding her. What had possessed her to rave on like that? The guy was a prince, for goodness' sake. He wasn't used to answering to anybody. What made her think she was so special that he'd actually give her an explanation for his strange behaviour?

'Goodbye, Natasha.'

Dante pushed away from the table and

inclined his head in her direction. She nodded back, aiming for the same polite little action, and knowing she probably ended up looking like Noddy on fast-forward.

He hesitated for a fraction and their gazes locked, hers enquiring and hopeful, his dark and unreadable, before he turned and walked out of her life.

Dante forced himself to walk out of the café and not look back, despite every instinct urging him to run back in there, sweep Natasha into his arms and never let go.

He hadn't expected to see her again. He'd planned on leaving a terse note along with the cheque for her to collect at the hotel once he'd gone.

After stewing all night, he'd finally managed to get his frustration under control and knew the best thing would be to change hotels. He'd had six days of blessed anonymity, and now he couldn't stay at Telford Towers for the next week, seeing her, running into her, having to pretend that everything was fine between them, when every time he closed his eyes the image of her in the arms of her ex flashed before him like some awful clip of a natural disaster.

It had been a simple plan, one that would've

been executed to perfection if he hadn't had a hankering for one last cup of espresso, and hadn't chosen the same café Natasha obviously frequented.

She must be a regular, judging by the old man's reaction when she'd walked in, but Dante couldn't fathom his own response. He'd invited her to sit down when it was the last thing he wanted, yet the minute he'd seen her he'd wanted to talk to her, to give her a chance to explain.

But he couldn't do it.

He couldn't ask her.

Maybe he was a proud man, maybe he was stubborn like his mother always said, but when she'd sat opposite him, looking cool and fresh in a strapless summer dress the colour of ripe watermelon, he'd lost it.

He'd wanted to demand answers, to discover why she still loved her ex despite telling him otherwise, why she didn't feel more for him, why she didn't feel the connection.

He'd wanted to touch her, to taste her full lips that matched her dress in colour perfectly, to run his fingers through her silky hair and savour her light floral fragrance.

He'd wanted her.

He'd wanted it all.

Instead, he'd sat there consumed by a cold,

hard rage, that a man who could have anything he wanted in this world couldn't have her.

He'd done the only thing possible: shut down emotionally, maintained a frosty façade, while anger at the futility of it all had bubbled hot and searing beneath the surface.

She could've said anything, done anything, and he wouldn't have reacted. He couldn't. He'd learned a long time ago the only way to deal with hardship, with disappointment, was to shut down.

This defence mechanism had served him well before and would now.

It was his way, the royal way.

Natasha sat in frozen silence, her fingers clasped so tight together she didn't register the pain of her fingernails digging into her flesh till Luigi placed a steaming mocha-cappuccino in front of her.

'Your young man left? What a pity,' he said, the old man's black eyes twinkling in his podgy face.

Luigi loved gossip almost as much as Ella, but right now she had no intention of becoming fodder for the rumour mill.

'He had to go. Thanks for the coffee; smells fabulous as usual.'

Luigi was also a sucker for flattery and, predictably, he preened like a proud peacock before bestowing a huge smile and strutting away.

Leaving her exactly where she'd been a few seconds ago: alone, bereft and shattered.

She didn't understand Dante's behaviour, any of it. From the time he'd strolled into the hotel and enlisted her help, none of it had made sense.

Though it was useless to ponder that now. She was more interested in his current abrupt turnaround—from welcoming her into his family one night to walking out on her the next morning without as much as a 'this is the reason why'.

Uh-uh, no sense at all.

He sure hadn't acted as if he'd been expecting her, either—the whole lack of warmth thing had been a dead giveaway! So, if she hadn't craved a mocha-cappa and dropped in at Trevi's, would he have even said goodbye?

If his icy demeanour had been any indication, she seriously doubted it.

Shaking her head, Natasha took a soothing sip of her cappuccino, savouring the creamy coffee sliding down her throat, enjoying the kick of caffeine.

Nothing made sense, least of all the empty sadness clawing at her soul, the devastation that indicated she felt a lot more for Dante than she'd let herself believe.

After another soothing sip, she spied the folded piece of paper on the table. Reaching across, she picked up the small rectangle and unfolded it, knowing it was a cheque. However, what did surprise her, what in fact shocked her, was the amount.

Enough money to clear her debt with Clay, to set her free, to set her family free.

Stifling the insane urge to giggle, she refolded the cheque and slipped it into her handbag. She could tear it up, but couldn't afford to let pride get in the way of common sense.

She'd wished for a miracle last night, had even considered approaching Dante for help, and ironically it looked like she'd got exactly what she'd hoped for.

Then why did it feel like the price she'd paid to gain her miracle was heartbreakingly high?

# CHAPTER TWELVE

'SEEING you twice in less than twenty-four hours—you sure you still haven't got a thing for me?'

Natasha heard the click of the door behind her and wondered if it was too late to make a bolt after Clay's secretary.

If his smarminess had made her skin crawl last night, seeing him again so soon made her want to retch.

Ignoring his pathetic greeting, she said, 'Thanks for seeing me. I have something for you.'

She kept her tone brisk, businesslike. She had to, otherwise she'd scream at him.

'This sounds promising.'

He didn't stand. Instead, he leaned back in his gigantic director's chair, hands clasped behind head, smug smile firmly in place, surrounded by a plush office backed by a million-dollar view.

She'd once been impressed by this: his status in the business world, his confidence, his suave looks. But now she saw it for what it was, a set of fake props for a con man. The type of man who would set out to make an innocent woman fall in love with him all in an attempt to get his hands on one of Melbourne's premier hotels.

Clay could've gone for any other hotel—he already owned a number of them—but he'd had to have the best, the crowning glory, the hotel which had been in a family for generations. So he'd set out to get his grubby hands on Telford Towers the only way he knew how.

By deception.

'I've got the final payment for you and the contract for you to sign off.'

'You're kidding?'

His cocky grin slipped, only to be replaced by a cruel twist of his thin lips.

'I'm not in the mood for jokes.' *Especially considering I'm looking at one.* 'Here. Sign next to the cross.'

'The hotel's floundering. How did you get the money so quickly?'

Forcing a sickly sweet smile, knowing it would infuriate him further, she said, 'That's none of your business. Now, sign along the dotted line like we agreed and let's put this all behind us.'

Clay's eyes narrowed to nasty slits as he suddenly bolted upright, his hands slamming on the monstrous mahogany desk.

'You weren't supposed to make the final payment. You were supposed to lose the lot, to me!'

Revulsion rose like acid bile in her throat, and she swallowed with effort. She'd suspected someone had been undercutting their supplies and interfering behind the scenes with the running of the Towers and, as much as she'd seen Clay's hand in it, hearing the man she'd once been engaged to admit his treachery made her physically ill.

'It was always about the Towers, wasn't it?'

The sneer on his face was more eloquent than any words. 'If you'd married me like you were supposed to, none of this would've happened. I'd be the current owner of your pathetic little family hovel, you'd still be running around like an errand girl, we'd have been happy. You wouldn't have had to pay back the money I gave you, I wouldn't have threatened to run a smear campaign on the hotel. Instead, you had to make a big song and dance about discovering my girlfriend, I told you a few home truths, and look where we ended up. Squabbling like a couple of kids.'

She knew the exact moment he'd give it one last go, the sly gleam of cunning lending his opaque eyes a demonic edge. A desperate man tried desperate means, and she knew what was coming before the slime ball opened his mouth.

'Come on, babe. We can give it one last try. Let's put all this behind us and start afresh. You know we'd be a dynamite team in the hotelier field, the best in the business. What do you say?'

*Drop dead?*

*Bite me?*

A whole host of less polite responses sprung to mind, but Natasha swallowed them all.

While her feet itched to turn around and make a run for the door, she stood still and tapped the contract in front of him.

'As you can see, this is a legally binding document. It states that my debt to you is paid off, that there will be no further business between us. Is that clear?'

He stood up so quickly she took a step back, hating the glitter of triumph in his cold eyes at a sign of her weakness.

'What if I don't sign? What if I instigate that smear campaign just as I threatened before, and drag your precious family through the mud?'

It took every ounce of self control for

Natasha not to pick up the nearest paperweight and throw it at him.

'You will sign, and you can keep your empty threats. You want to play dirty? Go ahead and try me.'

His sneer solidified her resolve to rid herself of this slime once and for all. 'What are you going to do?'

Clenching her hands into fists, she said, 'Fight back. The only reason I let you get away with any of this is because of my mother. You knew about her heart condition, you knew she was a worrier who'd been advised to avoid stress, but what do you do? You ram the fact you loaned us money down our throats and that you wanted it paid back in blood.'

Her voice choked with raw emotion, the devastation of losing her mum bubbling to the surface, the cold, hard rage that he'd been the cause of it all.

Taking a step forward, she jabbed a finger in his direction. 'You killed her. With your pathetic ruse to get your grubby hands on the hotel through me and your outrageous demands for payback with interest. You rubbed our noses in it, rubbed her nose in it, and you killed her, you bastard.'

His jaw dropped, and if she wasn't so furious

she would've laughed at his shock. 'Well, guess what? The damage is done. I've lost my mother, so any smear campaign you run now can't hurt her. I gave into your demands for her sake, to avoid further scandal ruining her health. But that's a moot point now. Go ahead, do your worst. The Telford name can hold its own, but can the same be said for your precious ego? You want me to tell the whole of Melbourne how you really do business and ruin your reputation? Go ahead and try me.'

'No one will believe you.'

She towered over him, wishing she could take a swing, knowing she'd never give him the satisfaction.

'You really take me for a fool, don't you? I have documents stating the original loan amount and the cashed cheque details made out to you. Everyone will know you're a shark, a greedy, manipulative user. So just keep my little proof in mind if you feel the urge to open that big mouth of yours and slander my hotel.'

As Clay's cheeks turned puce with rage, she tapped the contract. 'Sign here. I don't have all day.'

She knew she had him.

His threats might have frightened her at the start, when she would've done anything to save her family the pain of living through the mess she'd made, but not any more. She'd lost her mum, she'd lost her pride and she'd almost lost the hotel courtesy of trusting the wrong man.

But she'd repaid her debt, every last cent, she'd once seen as a generous handout from a caring fiancé who had strutted into her life with pledges of love and endless devotion. Of course, the scheming lowlife had demanded full payment plus interest when she'd ended their engagement, and she'd agreed to his terms for the sake of her family.

Now, Clay wouldn't bother her again. He had an enormous ego and valued appearances beyond anything; he would never risk his society cronies or his business associates finding out what he'd done to her. Making her repay a debt was one thing, charging her interest to stop him ruining her family via slander in the hotel business another.

Finally, she'd repaid every penny of his exorbitant interest charges, and as he picked up a silver pen, signed the contract and turned his back on her, she was free.

Folding the contract and tucking it into her purse, she headed for the door and didn't look back.

In fact, she held her head high and practically floated from the Collins Street skyscraper, intent on putting as much distance between Clay and her past as possible.

However, her elation lasted all of two seconds as she boarded a tram, took a seat and glanced out the window at the stunning Sofitel hotel, one of her major competitors, and spotted a familiar figure standing beside a gleaming silver stretch-limo.

Dante hadn't left.

She had to assume he'd merely changed hotels, given that the valet was opening the door for him and doffing his hat.

If he hadn't left the country as she'd thought, he'd changed hotels because he couldn't stand to be near her. It was the only explanation that made any sense.

Tears flooded her eyes and she blinked them away. She must've made a mistake. It wasn't Dante.

But as she watched a broad-shouldered guy in a designer suit, his too-long hair now trimmed to within an inch of its life, his too-blue eyes fixed on a thick pile of documents in his hands, she had her answer.

Dante had resumed his princely duties. He'd returned to normality, to his usual life which didn't include her. Seeing him dressed to the nines, clean shaven and short haired, merely reinforced that the guy she'd known didn't exist.

He never had.

He'd been trying to escape his life for whatever reasons and she'd got caught in the crossfire. Stupidly, irrevocably, caught in the crossfire which had wounded her heart along the way.

Watching the limo pull away, she swiped at her eyes and sank back into her seat.

Dante had left.

He'd left her.

And, for a woman who'd learned to cope with whatever traumas life threw her way, it hurt more than she could've imagined.

'He's left? What do you mean he's left?'

Natasha took a deep breath, not in the mood to placate Gina who bristled like an angry porcupine, her dark curly hair spiking in all directions as she leaned over the concierge's desk.

'But he told me he was staying here! Why would he change hotels?'

Natasha had pondered that very fact on the interminable tram ride home, grateful when she'd arrived back at the hotel to find she had to fill in for a shift. Anything to dull the pain of realising Gina must've been right. Dante had only been after one thing and, when she'd been too slow in producing the goods, he'd decided to cut his losses and run. Who knew, maybe he was over at the Sofitel right now buttering up some other gullible female with his sexy smile and piercing eyes.

'I have no idea,' she said, sending Gina a glare which said 'don't push me, lady, I'm not in the mood'.

Right now, she was beyond reason. She should've been doing cartwheels through the hotel foyer after finally getting rid of Clay. Instead, she wanted to rant and rave and scream at the injustice of losing the man she'd fallen for. She didn't need to face up to his sister when Gina was the last person she wanted to see.

'But you're his friend. Surely he would've given you some idea why he changed hotels?'

Gritting her teeth in frustration, Natasha said, 'I'm not your brother's keeper. I provided a service for him while he stayed here, that was all. If you need to speak to him, try ringing him.'

Though she wouldn't get the location of his new hotel from Natasha. She'd gone through enough trouble for the royal heartbreaker and being sued because she leaked information was more than she was willing to do.

'This is all very strange.' Gina fixed her with a suspicious glare, as if she didn't believe a word Natasha was saying. 'Dante doesn't do anything impulsively. His official hotel residence was scheduled here months ago. I can't understand why he'd up and leave, especially without telling me.'

Natasha refrained from rolling her eyes, just. If Gina didn't understand the workings of Dante's mind, what hope did she have? Trying to figure out how he might think was a total waste of time.

'If you want answers, the only way to get them is to ask Dante.' *And leave me alone!* 'I'm sorry I can't be of more assistance.'

'Perhaps I should be saying the same to you.'

Gina's dark eyes took on a speculative gleam and Natasha backed away, not liking where this was going.

'I don't know what you mean.'

Gina waved a bejewelled hand in front of her face. 'I'm not blind or stupid, despite what my brother might think of me. I may have made some silly decisions with my own life, but that doesn't mean I can't see what's going on with his.'

She leaned closer and dropped her voice to a dramatic whisper. 'Dante likes you. He would never have brought you to my home otherwise.

And, by the look of your long face, I'd say you're just as confused as me by his departure.'

Natasha stiffened, despising herself for the surge of hope Gina's words elicited. Dante liked her? Yeah, right, that was why he'd high-tailed it out of there without an explanation, leaving so fast her head still spun.

Keeping her voice steady with effort, Natasha said, 'Dante's departure has nothing to do with me. Now, if you don't mind, I have work to do—'

'Dante is a proud man, a stubborn man. Don't let his casual attire this last week fool you. He is regal to the bone, and if you want answers you'll have to go straight to the source.'

'I'm not going to see Dante!'

Damn it, the words popped out of her mouth before she could stop them, and Gina's gaze glittered with triumph. 'I can see his interest isn't one-sided. You have feelings for him too.'

Natasha shook her head, wishing her brain hadn't gone into overdrive at Gina's suggestion.

What if the woman was right? She could waste hours, days, longer, wondering why Dante left and why he lied about it. She was a worrier just like her mum; it was an integral part of her personality and she couldn't shut it off.

She'd worried about what her family would think of her hasty engagement to Clay.

She'd worried about taking money from her fiancé when the hotel hit a really tight spot.

She'd worried about losing the family business being her fault.

And now this.

In the grand scheme of things, her interlude with Dante should mean nothing. She should be able to move on, forget about him, chalk up her foolish crush to a woman whose self-esteem had taken a battering and who'd fallen for the next nice guy to smile her way.

However, what she'd shared with Dante hadn't been nothing. It had been something. A big something that kept her awake at night dreaming the impossible dream.

'You know I'm right,' Gina said, her tone surprisingly gentle. 'Go see him.'

She needed answers.

She needed closure.

She needed some sort of reassurance that what they'd shared hadn't been entirely in her imagination. If her self-esteem had been butchered by Clay, it would be nothing on the realisation that she'd conjured up some imaginary bond with Dante to soothe her weary soul.

How pathetic could a girl get?

Suddenly, Gina flung her hands in the air with typical Italian flamboyance. 'You're in love with him!'

Natasha stared at Gina in open-mouthed shock. 'What?'

'You heard me.'

Yeah, she'd heard her, and apart from being stunned by the words themselves she couldn't believe a woman she barely knew, a woman who had warned her off falling for her brother, had uttered them.

'You don't know anything about me,' she said, covering her discomfort with a fake chuckle. 'And I must say, coming hot on the heels of you warning me off Dante, it sounds rather hilarious, not to mention presumptuous.'

Gina reached out as if to grab her hand and Natasha scuttled back, wondering if her day— her week—could get any crazier. 'I'm sorry for what I said to you at Paolo's party. I love my brother and I'm protective of him. He has a hard life and I didn't want it to get harder if he fell for the wrong woman.' She shook her head. 'I can see I'm too late.'

'There is nothing between Dante and me.' She kept her voice steady with extreme effort, trying to project enough force without knocking the other woman down. Besides, what had she meant 'the wrong woman'?

This had to stop. She didn't have to stand here and listen to this.

'I think you should go.'

Her harsh tone should've convinced Gina to leave her alone but it didn't work. She merely stood there with a sorrowful expression on her expertly made-up face. Damn it, the woman had a hide like a rhinoceros.

'Deny it all you like. I know my brother and I can see it in your eyes. You cannot hide it.'

Great, now Gina subscribed to her 'eyes the window to the soul' motto too. 'Well? Are you in love with him?'

She couldn't love Dante.

She may be many things but she wasn't a complete fool. Falling in love with a bad boy would be crazy, falling in love with a rebel prince from the other side of the planet insane. He had a country to run, a suitable bride already chosen and waiting for him back home. She couldn't interfere with that even if she did love him.

Suddenly, an image flashed across her mind of her Dante with his too-long hair, dark stubble and sexy smile, trussed up like she'd seen him in his Internet photo and standing next to a princess. Another Dante altogether, a fake Dante, a Dante who wasn't hers.

Spots swam before her eyes and she gulped for air, hating the constricting band tightening around her chest, leaving her breathless and woozy.

And that's when it hit her.

She wanted *her* Dante, the guy she knew, the guy she'd fallen for, and she wanted him all for herself.

She did love him.

Heart and soul.

The kind of love that lingered long after the person had left your life, the kind of love you remembered for ever, that lasted for ever, no matter how much you tried to forget.

Natasha blinked several times, somewhat surprised to find Gina staring at her with concern, a concierge desk between them in a room where she'd sought refuge so many times over the last few years.

Her hotel's foyer, with its familiar ochre and red swirly rugs, its chocolate-brown suede couches and a hand-carved wooden chest her mum had given her for her twenty-first taking pride of place at the entrance to her office.

Other mums would've called it a glory box and hinted at a future of wedded bliss for their daughters, but not her mum. Her chest had been stuffed with her favourite things: a hand-made quilt, one of her mum's best patterns, with red Chinese silk alternating with gold, five boxes of her favourite caramels, the entire collection of Robbie Williams CDs, and a jade Buddha for good luck.

Her mum had been the best and she missed her terribly. Every time she snuggled up in the quilt she felt secure, as if her mum was right there, wrapping her arms around her along with the silky comforter.

What would her mum think of Dante?

She'd always had a thing for royalty, and Natasha remembered staring through the banisters of the hotel as a little girl, mesmerised by a visiting Asian king and queen that her mum had spun fantastic tales about.

Yeah, her mum would probably have liked Dante, but would she recommend her only child taking a chance on love knowing it could only lead to heartache?

'You don't have to say a word. Your face says it all.' Gina reached over the desk and patted her on the shoulder. 'Go and see him. It's the only way.'

The fool's way.

The dreamer's way.

Right now, she was a combination of both. She'd spent her life living up to responsibility, taking control of what needed to be done.

Well, she was tired of all that. Maybe it was foolish, maybe dreams were for suckers, but facing up to the truth after hearing it from a woman she barely knew had been the wake-up call she needed.

'I guess I should be thanking you, but I'm too busy blaming you.'

'What did I do?' Gina's tentative grin took years off her face, and Natasha could see a glimpse of the princess Dante had described, the type of woman who'd fallen for a foreign guy and had left her home to follow her dream.

If only she had the courage to do something like that…if only she had the opportunity…

'If you weren't so terrible at organising kids' parties, Dante wouldn't have needed my help and none of this would've happened.'

Gina shrugged, not at all insulted by her bluntness. 'I am a princess, what can I say?'

Natasha joined in her laughter, though it petered out quickly. No matter how she felt or whether she was willing to acknowledge it— let alone suss out how Dante felt—this couldn't end well.

There would be no happy endings here.

Dante had a country to run, she had a hotel to run.

They lived oceans apart.

And even if by some miracle he felt something for her, what did she think? That he'd ask her to be his princess?

Fat chance.

However, she needed to do this for herself, and confronting Dante would be the first step in getting over him.

*You wish.*

'I'm going to see him right now,' she said, frantically signalling at a front-desk employee to act as stand-in concierge before she changed her mind.

'Good.' Gina's smug grin annoyed her, and she fixed her with a glare.

'Why are you doing this?'

'Because I love Dante.' Well, that made two of them. 'I care about what happens to him.'

Though Natasha didn't have a sibling, she understood where Gina was coming from. If anyone ever messed with Ella, she would interfere too.

'If there's anything else I can do—'

'Please don't take this the wrong way, Gina, but I've listened to your crazy theories about me loving your brother.' *Well, not so crazy as it turned out.* 'And I've considered what you've said when I hardly know you, but I think I can take it from here.'

Could she say 'butt out' any more politely?

'I think that will change very soon—the part about you not knowing me,' Gina said, not fazed in the slightest by her outburst. 'Now, I must go. Tell the runaway his sister is looking for him and get him to call me? *Ciao.*'

Gina blew her a kiss and strolled across the lobby, looking every inch a princess in head-to-toe designer black.

She must be crazy to listen to his sister, a woman who the day before had been warning her to stay away.

She must be totally insane to consider confronting Dante after he'd made it perfectly clear he wanted nothing more to do with her.

Well, luckily for her, she was in a loco type of mood, and after the fastest handover in history she sprinted for her room.

'I'm not trying to impress him,' Natasha muttered, yanking her favourite black cargos and apple-green halter out of the wardrobe as she shimmied out of the boring navy suit she'd worn to her meeting with Clay. 'But I don't want to scare him off either.'

Besides, perhaps a change of outfit would give her a much needed boost in confidence.

Okay, now she was taking fashion advice from her inner voice, which just so happened to be making itself heard. Could she get any more pathetic?

Annoyed at her interior monologue, she dressed, slipped her feet into strappy high-heeled sandals and fastened small silver hoops in her ears, running a quick slick of gloss over her lips.

*Go get him, princess.*

While Natasha frowned at her frightened reflection, she couldn't help but like how the title sounded.

# CHAPTER THIRTEEN

TAKING a deep breath, Natasha knocked on the door of room 1718 before she lost her nerve.

Her sharp rapping at the door shattered the peace of the plush corridor with its soft lighting and thick carpet.

Maybe Dante wasn't in. She'd been so fired up to confront him and get this ordeal over and done with that she hadn't considered that scenario. Besides, her mind had been too busy devising a way to discover his room number when Lady Luck had smiled down on her. Running into Fay, the Sofitel's day manager and her one-time room-mate at an hotelier's conference, had been a major bonus.

She hadn't felt so great having to tell a little white lie to get the information she needed out of Fay. But, hey, the whole 'a client left something rather delicate behind at the Towers and I thought I'd bring it over and deliver it personally' story had been the most plausible thing she'd been able to come up with on the spur of the moment.

Thankfully, it had worked like a charm and Fay had given her Dante's room number—after ear-bashing her for ten minutes on how utterly dreamy the prince was. As if she hadn't noticed!

Glaring at the wooden door and wishing it would open, Natasha almost stumbled back when it did.

'What are you doing here?'

Okay, not the most pleasant of greetings, and Dante sure didn't look happy to see her if that massive frown and lack of a smile was any indication. Well, too bad. She hadn't come all this way to turn tail and run now.

'Can I come in?'

Calm, collected, straight to the point. If only she could keep it up, if he ever let her in the door.

'Fine, but I have a lot of work to do, so make it quick.'

He stepped aside and, ignoring his rudeness, she entered the room, her keen eye doing a quick scan of the competition. Larger than the Towers' average room, the Tiffany lamps, the comfy armchairs, the antiques and the fresh flowers all faded into oblivion when her gaze lit on the bed, a huge king-size monstrosity covered in the richest cream damask fabric. It appeared larger than life, and seemed to beckon with its plump cushions and thick quilt.

When the door shut, she quickly averted her gaze and swung around to face Dante, desperately trying to erase the vivid image she'd just had of the two of them together on that inviting bed.

'Would you like something to drink?'

'No thanks.'

'Why are you here, Natasha?'

Well, that took care of the formalities, but in a way she was glad he cut to the chase. She hadn't come here to rehash old news, she wanted answers, closure, anything to ease the tension winding her tighter than a spring.

'You said you were leaving. You're still here.'

A wary expression flickered in his eyes, the clear aquamarine highlighted by his pale blue business shirt, the faintest gold pinstripes catching the light. On anyone else, the shirt would've looked wrong. On him, it accentuated his status and screamed royalty.

By the rest of his outfit, it seemed he'd stepped back into prince mode well and truly: designer trousers with a perfect crease, the fancy shirt and a royal-blue tie bearing what looked like a small crest. Probably the Andretti coat of arms. He appeared all business, and then some, and she didn't like it.

Natasha had thought he might still be casual. The Dante she knew…and loved. However, there wasn't a peep of denim or stubble in sight, and she missed it, missed the warmth they'd once shared if for an all too brief moment.

Dante in his fancy outfit looked every inch the untouchable prince, and served to reinforce the huge gap between them. What hope did she have?

'But why are *you* here?'

She hated when people didn't give her direct answers or, worse, answered a question with a question. Her parents had raised her to be upfront and honest at all costs.

*Then why don't you go ahead and tell him why you're really here?*

Hmm…maybe her whole 'honesty is the best policy' motto could wait just a tad longer.

Trying not to shuffle under his steady stare, she thrust her hands in her pockets and squared her shoulders. 'Gina is looking for you.'

He raised an eyebrow, obviously not expecting that response. 'I'll get in touch with her. Now, if there's nothing else—'

'Actually, I wanted to clear the air between

us,' she rushed on, hating his stilted formality, wanting to recapture the closeness they'd had.

His frown deepened. 'We have nothing to discuss that I'm aware of.'

'Then we agree to differ. The way I see it, we were getting along just fine and then yesterday, out of the blue, you up and leave. Only you didn't leave Melbourne as you led me to believe, you changed hotels, which begs the question—why?'

'I don't owe you any explanations,' he said, staring over her shoulder at the stunning view of the Melbourne city skyline she'd glimpsed when she'd first entered the room.

'You're right, you don't owe me anything. But you're a decent guy and I thought we had a connection. The time we spent together seemed special, and perhaps there was something more than just friendship between us. Maybe I was wrong?'

There, she'd said it.

So the words had tumbled out in a confused jumble, and she'd spoiled the ending by her voice rising, but she'd made the first overture, had told the semi-truth—*'connection' could be a euphemism for love, right*? Now she waited, breath held, for some kind of response from the man who set her pulse pounding just by being in the same room.

He didn't flinch, he didn't move, he didn't speak, and for an endless, embarrassing moment Natasha thought she'd have to walk out the door with her pride as well as her heart in tatters.

Finally, something shifted in his eyes, cold wariness replaced by a flicker of warmth, and he gestured to the armchairs. 'Please be seated.'

Not exactly the answer she'd been hoping for, but it was a start. At least she was still here and, by his softening posture, she might get the answers she'd hoped for yet.

After folding his tall frame into the chair opposite, he sat back and regarded her with a suspicious stare.

'I didn't say I was leaving Melbourne. You chose to interpret it that way.'

'But why would you leave Telford Towers? I thought you liked it there from what you said, and after the time we spent together...' She trailed off, surprised by the sudden flash of fire in his eyes.

'That was a business arrangement.'

The fire she'd glimpsed quickly dimmed to glacial coldness, matching his icy, clipped tone.

'Which you reneged on!'

Wrong answer. He froze, his posture screaming 'back off'.

'Was the cheque not suitable?'

'The cheque was fine. In fact, it was very generous, but that's not what I meant and you know it.'

'I have other business to attend to this week and taking part in your hotel's publicity would not have fit in. I made a business decision, nothing personal.'

Right then, it hit her, and Natasha sagged against the plump cushions.

*Nothing personal...*

Unfortunately, that was the problem here. She'd obviously built a ludicrous fairy tale in her head about mutual attraction and friendship and camaraderie when in fact, from Dante's point of view, there had been nothing personal in any of it.

Nothing personal, indeed.

'I'm sorry to take up your time.' She rose, aiming for a dignified exit.

She'd come here for answers and she'd got what she wanted. Unfortunately, her heart refused to comprehend what her head had computed a long time ago: she wasn't cut out for relationships or whatever it was she thought she'd shared with Dante.

She didn't like pain, particularly the dull ache residing around her heart which would take a lifetime to shift. It wasn't an entirely new sensation. She'd felt something similar when she'd learned of Clay's betrayal, and later when her mum died, but the pain had been different. More acute, less pervasive.

Nothing like the building pressure, the constant ache, which centred around her heart now and spread its tentacles outwards, squeezing the very breath out of her.

She had to get out. Now.

Crossing the room took an eternity as she concentrated on forcing her feet to move, and she sighed in relief as her hand hit the cold door-handle.

'You lied too.'

Natasha stopped, her hand poised in mid-turn, not sure if she'd heard correctly.

'There couldn't have been any connection between us because you're still involved with your ex.'

Without thinking, she whirled to face him, her desperate escape plan thwarted by the urge to throw something at him.

'You're crazy. I loathe him. You saw how he was when you pulled your little stunt out the front of the Towers. Why would you think I'd still be involved with him?'

He folded his arms and glared, the epitome of a guy not used to being crossed.

'I saw you in the Lobby Bar. All over him.'

She shook her head, wishing she could take hold of his and knock it against the wall to bang some sense into him.

'That wasn't how it looked.'

Suddenly, Dante moved towards her in a blur, his hands gripping her upper arms so tight she almost cried out.

'You want to know how it looked? It looked like you were a cosy couple, that you were enjoying it, that you were the type of woman to flirt with one man and wrap him around your little finger for a week, while still involved with another.'

He spat the words out, his voice laced with contempt, his arms rigid, and as she stared into the furious face of the man she loved Natasha knew she finally had her closure.

'You saw what you wanted to see,' she said, breaking his hold and opening the door in record speed, hating the sobs which bubbled out of her throat, and tore free, dashing the tears from her eyes.

She may have fallen in love with a prince but Dante had just proved himself a lesser man than she'd thought.

'Tasha, I'm sorry—'

She didn't wait to hear the rest as the door

slammed shut and her feet flew down the long corridor.

She'd heard enough.

'What is troubling you?'

Dante turned from the parapet, not in the mood to have this conversation with his mother. Then again, he wasn't in the mood for much these days.

'Nothing,' he said, knowing she wouldn't leave it alone.

Elena Andretti, Queen of Calida, didn't disappoint.

'Ever since you returned from Melbourne yesterday, you look like the sky is going to fall in. Or, worse, that I'm going to announce your betrothal in your first week home.'

She crossed the ancient stone flag way and took hold of his hand, her grip as strong as ever. 'Please, give your old mother some credit. I'm going to wait till next week at least!'

He usually laughed at his mother's feeble jokes. Today, he couldn't even muster a half-hearted chuckle.

'What happened? Was it a woman?'

'It was nothing.' He shook his head, hating how insignificant that sounded.

Nothing…what a lie.

Natasha had been the woman with the potential to rock his world, and in many ways she had, yet no matter which way he looked at it the whole thing with her had been a sham. He'd seen the proof with his own eyes.

'If you don't tell me, Gina will.'

His mother dropped his hand and turned away, leaning on the parapet and taking in the view he'd just been staring at without seeing.

'I never tire of this view. The unique colour of the ocean, the fishing boats, the whitewashed houses, the mountains. We're blessed, Dante, to rule such beauty. It is a gift from God, and we can never take it for granted. You know that, don't you?'

Dante propped himself next to her, knowing this was yet another variation on her usual 'you are a man with responsibilities' speech, the same speech he'd heard in a thousand different ways since he'd been able to walk and talk.

'I don't need a lecture, Mother.'

She turned to face him with a surprising turn of speed for a woman who used an ornate cane to get anywhere these days, her gait usually a slow, regal shuffle.

'You need something to snap you out of this lethargy. It won't do for people to see you like this.'

'It's jetlag, that's all.'

Though he knew that excuse would soon wear thin. Somehow, he knew his lack of sleep on the long flight home and since his arrival had nothing to do with a haywire body clock and everything to do with a stunning brunette he couldn't get out of his mind.

'Well, see that you get enough rest. We're entertaining several prominent families over the next few evenings, starting tomorrow. You need to be at your best.'

Dante stifled a grimace, deciphering his mother's code easily. 'Entertaining prominent families' meant she'd chosen a selection of prospective brides and he'd be expected to make a decision before the week was out.

An appalling old tradition at the best of times, but now, with his head still spinning with memories of Natasha and his heart doing goodness knew what, he couldn't summon enthusiasm to get out of bed let alone entertain his future wife.

'It is your duty, Dante.'

With those ominous words ringing in his ears, he watched his mother walk away, an old lady in tailored finery but an old lady nonetheless.

He knew about duty.

He'd been born to it, raised to it.

He didn't have a choice.

But what if there was more to life?

He'd never questioned his birthright and, even while envying Gina her freedom to marry whomever she chose and live wherever took her fancy, he'd always known where his duty lay.

Meeting Natasha had changed all that.

For the first time in his life, he'd known what it felt like to belong, and it had nothing to do with location or possessions or home. Instead, it had everything to do with being with the right person, the type of person who made you laugh and smile and want to be a better man.

Unfortunately for him, he'd felt all that and more in less than a week of knowing her, a woman who belonged to another.

However, one thing still niggled: her visit to his hotel and the motivation behind her passionate outburst. He'd analysed it, considered it from every angle, and it didn't make sense.

She'd had no reason to visit him and accuse him of lying about leaving, even less reason to discuss the connection they'd shared. Her bluntness had surprised him, taken him off guard, but he'd quickly dismissed the whole thing as a desperate attempt on her part to get him involved in her hotel's publicity again.

However, she hadn't mentioned any of that. And when he'd lost his cool at the end about seeing her with her ex, the look of devastation in her eyes had nearly killed him. He's glimpsed raw, savage pain before she'd run away, her sobs tearing at his soul.

He'd almost run after her before his damned pride had kicked in.

She'd made her choice, who was he to interfere in her life? If anyone knew what that was like, he did.

His whole life had been open to scrutiny, available for anybody and everybody to interfere with. He'd accepted it a long time ago but that didn't mean he had to like it. He respected Natasha's freedom of choice, almost envied it, even if the thought of her with her ex made him want to jump off the castle.

*Why the visit?*

It all came back to the same question, reverberating around his head till he could quite happily thump it against the ancient stone parapet just to clear it.

She hadn't acted like a woman trying to stay close to him for the sake of business. In fact, the longer he pondered her motivation, the harder it was to shake off the conviction that she'd acted like a woman who cared. About him.

Ridiculous.

Wishful thinking?

Whatever, he needed to forget her.

He had a life of responsibility ahead of him, a life as a husband, a life as a king.

Starting tomorrow, he'd take the first step in doing the right thing, the honourable thing, the type of sacrifice expected of a ruler. He would choose a suitable bride and make the most of it, just like leaders of Calida had done for centuries before him.

Starting tomorrow...

For today, he would purge his mind of Natasha's memory as best he could.

And pray to God his future bride sparked as much passion, as much interest in him, as she had.

# CHAPTER FOURTEEN

'How's my favourite girl?'

Natasha looked up from the ledger she'd been poring over, smiling for the first time in a week.

'Welcome home, Dad.'

She flung herself into his arms as she had as a little girl, fast and furious, needing a comforting hug more now than she ever had back then.

'I take it you missed me?'

Roger Telford stepped out of her embrace, holding her at arm's length. 'If that's the type of welcome home I get, remind your dear old dad to go away more often.'

Natasha chuckled. 'You make it sound like I take you for granted when you're here.'

'Just kidding, princess.' He tapped her on the nose and sank into the nearest chair, patting the arm while her heart somersaulted.

She'd had a whole week to put the Dante

fiasco behind her, seven long days to concentrate on business, throw herself into making the hotel flourish now it was properly theirs again. One hundred and sixty eight endless hours to fill with girlie chats with Ella, work and sleep, anything to stop her thinking of Dante and how wrong she'd been about him.

And all it took was her dad to call her by an ancient pet name and it all flooded back, every embarrassing detail of how she'd virtually thrown herself at Dante and how he'd rebuked her.

'Is everything all right?'

Mustering a smile with effort, she said, 'Fine. And you will be too when I tell you my news.'

She needed to distract her dad, and quickly. Since the Clay debacle, he'd been extra protective and if he got a whiff there was something wrong—or worse, that it had to do with a man—he'd never drop it.

'What news?'

His jovial smile vanished, the wrinkles around his eyes deepening as he fixed her with a worried stare.

'It's good, Dad, and I didn't tell you while you were in Perth because I knew you'd probably fly straight back here.'

'This doesn't sound good. Now, sit down before I get a crick in my neck.'

Natasha perched on the chair's arm, remembering the many times she'd done the same thing growing up. Her parents had always had an open-door policy and, with Natasha being an only child, they'd been an incredibly close family.

She'd come to them when Debbie MacCraw had bullied her the first day of school, she'd come to them when Samuel Grace hadn't asked her to the graduation dance, and she'd come to them when she'd discovered Clay's true colours—lily-livered stripes.

However, no matter how understanding her dad would be, she'd save the Dante disaster for another day. He'd only just arrived home, and she'd make sure the news was all good.

'Relax, Dad. You're going to love this, I promise.' She patted his shoulder, surprised to feel the bony prominences under the thin cotton shirt.

Her dad had always been larger than life for her, as healthy as a horse, but when her mum had died she'd noticed a certain frailty about him and it looked like he hadn't been eating well while away.

'The Towers is ours again. One hundred percent debt free.'

'You paid that scumbag off? How?'

Rather than alleviating the lines around her dad's eyes, his frown increased them tenfold.

'The Prince of Calida helped. I did some PA work for him while he was here; he paid me well. It was a win-win situation for everyone.'

Then why did she feel like the biggest loser in the world?

'That is good news. I can't believe it.'

Her dad sat back, his frown disappearing, replaced by a stunned expression which took years off him. 'We're seriously debt free again?'

'Seriously.'

Natasha smiled, squeezed her dad's shoulder and stood up. Now that she'd delivered the good news, time for her to escape while her dad was still absorbing it. Otherwise, he'd turn his eagle eye back on her, and she couldn't stand the scrutiny right now. Who knew what she might blab under duress?

'Guess we owe the prince one.'

Her smile faltered but she recovered quickly. 'I thanked him. He was very impressed with our hotel. I'm sure he'll recommend us.'

As if.

He'd been so impressed he'd vacated quicker than she could say 'please come again,' and crossed town to the opposition.

'Have I told you lately what an asset you are to the hotel? And how lucky I am to have you as a daughter?'

His eyes misted over, and Natasha knew she'd have to make a run for it before she started blubbering.

'You don't have to tell me. I know. Now, you relax and I'll organise supper to be brought up to you.'

Her dad smiled. 'I am a bit tired. See you in the morning?'

'You bet.'

Blowing him a kiss, Natasha left the room where she'd spent her happiest years with her family. However, come morning, she wondered if the happy times would be a thing of the past once she dropped the next bombshell on her dad.

Natasha had just finished the new concierge's orientation when Gina walked into the hotel foyer, her searching gaze zoning in on Natasha before she could duck behind the front desk.

Great, just what she needed, a blast from the not-so-distant, not-so-pleasant past.

'Not you again!' She was *so* not in the mood for whatever the princess had to say.

Ignoring her blatant rudeness, Gina smiled.

'Just the woman I wanted to see. Do you have a minute?'

Natasha made a big show of checking her watch when she knew the only pressing engagement she had was with her dad to tell him her decision.

'One minute.'

Natasha indicated the comfy couches in a secluded corner of the lobby, and Gina nodded.

She looked amazing in a fitted burgundy coat-dress with matching designer handbag and shoes, her make-up immaculate, her curls in perfect smooth ringlets. Natasha felt like Orphan Annie in hand-me-downs next to her.

'If you've come here to talk about Dante again, forget it.' Natasha hated how rude she sounded, but she didn't care. She was over the Andretti family, well and truly.

Gina sighed and shook her head. 'Did Dante tell you about our mother?'

Natasha wondered if she'd entered the twilight zone. Every time Gina showed up and opened her mouth, her confusion meter went up a notch.

'A bit.'

'Mother is pushy, opinionated and always right.'

'Hmm…' Natasha mumbled, stifling a grin

as she recalled Dante saying something along similar lines about Gina.

'Dante's life has been mapped out since birth, whereas I had the fortune to be born a girl, and second, so I could escape. My brother hasn't had the privilege.'

Everything was still clear as mud, so Natasha opted for her usual honest policy.

'I'm not sure why you're telling me all this.'

With a swift change in mood that left Natasha reeling, Gina's dark eyes pinned hers with an accusatory glare. 'Dante didn't say goodbye to me, he simply vanished back home. He isn't taking my calls either. Normally I wouldn't interfere any more than I already have, but this is getting out of control. Apparently, he's behaving like a love-struck fool in Calida. My mother is at her wits' end and she's pestering me every day to find out what happened when Dante was in Melbourne. I had to see you and find out how your last visit went with Dante before my mother drives me mad. Or worse, visits me.'

Gina paused to take a breath while Natasha tried to ignore the fact of Dante in love with some lucky woman.

*Love-struck…love-struck…*

The phrase made her head ache, and froze her heart in a veneer of icy misery.

It shouldn't hurt this much.

She should be over him.

She'd tried everything, from distracting visualisation techniques—somehow, a calm beach scene morphed into her and Dante frolicking in the waves together—to rainforest CDs—the soothing bird chirps reminded her of animals, which reminded her of Dante and their visit to the animal farm.

On and on it went: the memories of the loaded stares and that scintillating kiss, fake or not. She couldn't get him out of her head, and now Gina had to show up to rub her nose in it. What was with this family?

Natasha stood and towered over Gina, trying to make a point with her intimidating stance. 'Look, I'm happy for Dante, but I have no idea why your mother is hounding you or why in turn you're hounding me. You don't even know me!'

Gina's perfectly shaped eyebrows shot up. 'You're happy he's pining over you? Aren't you going to do something about it?'

Natasha sat down as quickly as she'd stood up. 'You can't possibly mean—'

'Come on, you don't need to play games with me any more. We both know he's totally in love with you but for some reason you're here while he's there. I'd hoped maybe you'd sorted out something. Maybe you're going to join him shortly?'

Natasha wanted to strangle the woman. However, if she did that, she'd never get to the bottom of this whole mix-up. For some bizarre, twisted reason, Gina thought Dante was in love with her.

She wished.

Knowing it would take the blunt truth to get rid of Gina, Natasha said, 'Dante and I didn't part on the best of terms after *you* prompted me to go see him. And I can categorically say I'm the last person he'd be in love with. So there's been a mistake, and I'm sorry, but you'll have to sort it out yourselves.'

Gina shook her head, her slick curls tumbling around her heart-shaped face. 'No mistake. Dante loves you.'

Natasha sat back in an undignified slump, despising herself for the surge of hope Gina's words fuelled.

Dante loved her? No way.

They'd definitely had a spark, but he'd even denied that when she'd confronted him, when she'd put her heart on the line and he'd trampled it without a thought.

She'd harboured a faint hope he might've cared more than he was letting on when he'd been jealous about seeing her with Clay, but that hope had soon faded into oblivion around the time he'd let her walk out of his life without giving her a chance to explain, or putting up a fight.

Uh-uh, he couldn't love her.

He didn't love her.

*But what if he did?*

Gina snapped her fingers like a conjurer creating magic. 'You should go visit him in Calida. Sort everything out. Stay there. Get married. Whatever. Just be gentle. Dante's a good man and he deserves to be happy.'

Natasha stared at Gina as if she'd lost her mind. 'I can't. I put myself on the line with your brother once, he didn't want me. End of story.'

'That's what you think,' Gina said, leaping up from the chair as if she'd sat on an ant hill. 'I was wrong about you. You weren't a last fling for my brother, you're the only woman he wants.'

Natasha shook her head, formulating another argument to convince Gina she'd lost her mind. However, she never had a chance as Gina bent to give her a quick hug, muttered 'I'll be in touch' and stormed away before she could say another word.

This can't be happening, Natasha thought, while a glimmer of an idea flickered in the far recesses of her brain. The news she had to tell her dad involved a break. A much needed break from the hotel, a little R and R, a chance to regroup her thoughts, heal her heart.

She'd planned on taking a mini holiday. Somewhere warm, remote, secluded, with little interference from the outside world. A small island, perhaps?

No, no, no!

Gina had messed with her head. She had no intention of visiting Calida, now or ever.

If her self-esteem had taken a battering with Clay, it had fractured for ever with Dante. She didn't need him reinforcing how he didn't find her appealing, how much she'd got the whole situation skewed. She may be many things, but a masochist wasn't one of them.

Her plan was simple.

Now that her dad was back, she could take a well-earned break and figure out where her life was heading. She'd invested most of her life in the hotel, and suddenly its dazzle had worn off. Whether the lure of the unobtainable fairy tale or meeting a go-get-'em guy like Dante had tainted her view, she knew it was time to take stock.

And banish thoughts of a blue-eyed sexy prince from her mind for ever.

* * *

'You've been avoiding me.'

Dante sat behind his desk, used to facing pushy dignitaries and world leaders via the wonders of tele-conferencing, but never had he faced an irate Gina.

His sister looked mad enough to jump on a plane and return to Calida, and that was saying something.

'I haven't been avoiding you. I just didn't have time to say goodbye in Melbourne and I've been very busy since I returned home.'

'Liar,' she said, her black eyes flashing with disgust clearly visible even on a grainy screen. 'You were never any good at telling lies.'

'A good thing, I would suggest.' He sat back and folded his arms, wishing he wasn't so defensive around her all the time.

He'd always been like this with his younger sister: vacillating between condescending and superior, firm and in charge. He couldn't help it. Once his father had died, he'd become the man of the family, his mother had seen to that.

In a way, he felt like he'd failed Gina in not protecting her better from her disastrous marriage, in not making her understand the beauties of home. Maybe if he'd done a better job looking after his sister, she wouldn't have done absolutely anything—including marrying the wrong man—to escape.

'Cut the smug act, big brother. I need to discuss something important with you.'

He sat forward, concerned. 'Are you all right? Is Paolo all right?'

He was so wrapped up in his misery that perhaps he'd missed something.

'We're fine, though we're both hurting from you running out on us without saying goodbye.'

Dante flinched as if she'd reached through the screen and struck him. He hated how he'd left without talking to his family, especially when he'd specifically travelled to Melbourne earlier to rebuild bridges with his sister.

But he couldn't face her after the debacle with Natasha, couldn't face her inevitable probing, her bossy brand of curiosity, so he'd taken the easy way out and had withdrawn into official duties. For Gina to talk about emotions, he must've hurt her beyond belief. His super-confident sister never thought of anyone's feelings let alone her own.

'I'm sorry. I had a lot on my mind.'

'I know. I visited her. Twice.'

He sat up and peered at the screen. 'I beg your pardon?'

Gina smiled, the same cheeky smile she'd

given him a thousand times growing up, when she'd put snails in his bed, snatched the last sweet cannoli off his plate, and fed his algebra to a goat.

'Natasha. Your *friend*. I've seen her, twice.'

His heart flipped at hearing her name, his mind blurring with images of her and the special time they'd spent together in a city far away.

'Why would you do something like that? You don't even know her.'

'So she keeps telling me.' Gina rolled her eyes. 'She's as stubborn as you, that one. You're a match made in heaven.'

'You didn't answer my question,' he said, ignoring the stab of pain lancing his soul. Perhaps they could've been a good match if only Natasha had been more honest with him and he was a different man.

'I'm doing this because I want you to be happy,' she said, her voice dropping unexpectedly. 'Because I don't want you making the same mistakes I did.'

Damn it, they should've been having this talk face to face, not via nebulous technological means. He'd screwed up with his sister—again.

'Are you sure you want to talk about this?'

Gina nodded, her dark curls bouncing

around her face. 'Don't you think we've avoided it for too long?'

She was right, but was this the time or place? His mind was in a muddle over Natasha and his emotions swinging all over the place.

After a long moment, he finally nodded. 'You know I love you, right?'

Her bittersweet smile spoke volumes. 'Yes, but you also resent me. You always have.'

An instant rebuttal sprung to his lips and he swallowed it. As much as it pained him to admit it, she was right, and he'd fostered this latent animosity long enough.

'I've envied your freedom, your ability to take charge of your own destiny,' he said, hating how petty he sounded but feeling like a weight had slipped off his shoulders for admitting it.

'Even when I made a mess of things?'

'At least it was your choice to make. I may have come across as the disapproving brother, but that's only because of my own inadequacies at not protecting you better. Besides, you're happy now?'

Gina's genuine smile warmed his heart better than any confession. 'I love Melbourne. Don't tell Mother, but I'm proud to be Calidian and I even miss home at times. Though I wouldn't trade my current life for the world...or a crown,' she added, a pointed glance his way, which lost some of its impact through the screen.

'Don't get carried away. I may envy you your freedom, but my duty is important to me. It's what I've grown up with, it's what I know, and I'd never let my country down.'

'But what about yourself?'

Her almost whisper slammed into his conscience, resurrecting similar questions he'd asked himself but successfully buried when he'd put his interlude with Natasha behind him.

'I am content,' he said, hating how hollow his forced statement sounded.

His sister finally sounded at peace and they'd broached their feelings; the last thing he wanted to do was laden her down with his problems.

'Content is not happy. Content does not recognise love. Content does not keep you warm at night or stand by your side while you rule.'

'Leave it alone, Gina.'

He had, leaving his brief taste of true happiness behind when he closed his heart to the one woman who made him dream about possibilities and future.

Gina smiled and waggled her finger at him. 'Now, what sort of a caring sister would I be if I left you to your own devices? What I wanted to say before we got all sentimental was that Natasha is in love with you, so whatever is keeping you apart get over it and make yourself happy for once. Calida will always be there, the crown will always be there, but your one shot at true love may not be, so don't screw it up.'

She didn't have to add 'like I did'. He could see regret written all over her face.

Not wanting to hurt his sister after she'd gone to a lot of trouble to finally pin him down and open up, he said, 'I appreciate all of this.'

Non-committal, honest and brief, his usual way of handling news which made him uncomfortable. And right now the thought of Natasha truly loving him and the fact he'd thrown it away didn't only make him uncomfortable, it made him downright sick to his stomach.

'Good luck, big brother.'

Gina blew him a kiss and he returned the action, feeling exceedingly stupid sending kisses to a screen.

Not half as stupid as he'd feel if he'd managed to ruin any chance of a future with the woman he loved.

# CHAPTER FIFTEEN

'YOU sure you want to do this?'

Natasha zipped her case, plopped onto the bed next to her dad and slipped an arm around his waist. 'I'm sure, though I'm going to miss you.'

'Bet you won't even give us a second thought.'

Ella leaned in the bedroom doorway, a mutinous frown on her expressive face, the same kind of look Natasha had seen a million times when Ella was trying to contain her emotions. No way would her feisty friend ever let anyone see her cry.

'I'm taking a break, not leaving for ever. Come on, guys, be happy for me.'

Her dad hugged her. 'We are, sweetheart. It just won't be the same around here without you. But take as long as you like. We'll be fine.'

'Yeah,' Ella said, swiping a hand over her eyes at the same time she did. 'Jinx!'

For Natasha's sake, she could do without any jinxes. She needed a change of luck, starting today.

'Right. Time to go.'

She hated goodbyes for the simple fact she'd never had to face many. A homebody all her life, she'd loved the Towers too much to leave, loved her family too much to be away for longer than school camp. Familiarity bred security, and right at that moment, surrounded by her dad and her best friend, she'd never felt so secure.

But she was a big girl now.

Time to shake her life up a little, step out of her comfort zone and give her self-esteem a much-needed boost—starting with a month-long sojourn on one of Australia's northern-most beaches.

'Love you, Dad,' she said, succumbing to her dad's bear hug and blinking back tears.

'Love you too, princess,' he said, ruffling her hair like he had when she was four, and making her want to bawl more than ever.

Pulling away, she turned towards Ella with arms outstretched. 'Hug me if you think I'm cool.'

Ella snorted and, as she hugged her tight, she knew she couldn't have survived the last few years without her, and hoped her extended break wouldn't change things between them. They were more than best friends; Ella had become her surrogate sister, and she needed her as much as her dad.

'Enough of the mushy stuff,' Ella said, breaking the hug as both of them made surreptitious sweeps at their eyes.

A loud knock at the door startled Natasha and she glanced at her watch. 'Must be the bell boy. Okay, load up the bags. Looks like I'm on my way.'

Ella opened the door while she bustled around the room, making sure she hadn't left anything behind.

'Anyone seen my Palm Pilot?'

An eerie silence greeted her and she swung around, wondering if the others had ducked out on her rather than face any more goodbyes.

However, Ella and her dad hadn't left. Instead, they surrounded the open doorway like a welcoming committee while a guy wearing a uniform—not one of the hotel's— slowly turned around.

Natasha's heart stopped and she held her breath, her head reeling from lack of oxygen or shock, or a combination of both, as she stared in open-mouthed amazement at the last man she'd ever expected to see.

'We'll leave you alone,' Ella said, herding her confused dad out the door and closing it behind them in record time.

'Hello, Tasha.'

'What are you doing here?'

To her surprise, she managed to work her mouth and brain in sync, though now her heart had kick-started again the roaring of her pulse in her ears almost deafened her.

'I'm here on official business.'

Dante hadn't moved far into the room, giving her plenty of opportunity to study him. She'd never seen him like this: navy uniform, myriad medals pinned over his left breast pocket, hair slicked back without a curl in sight. However, what threw her the most was his expression: uncertainty warred with hope, warmth battled with—dare she say it?—desire.

'Official business, huh?'

He nodded, a stilted action which fitted perfectly with his formal attire, a regal action befitting a prince.

'Yes. I've come to apologise for my atrocious behaviour when we last met. And to convince the woman I love to take a chance on me. A very important task I couldn't entrust to anybody else, so here I am.'

Natasha gaped, knowing he couldn't possibly

mean what he'd just said, knowing he couldn't possibly be referring to her.

'Well?'

Suddenly, her brain kicked into gear and she snapped out of the befuddled fog that had pervaded the room the minute he'd stepped into it.

'Well what? You expect me to believe that? Come on, I'm not that gullible.'

She folded her arms and propped on the hall table, wishing her pulse would slow down, wishing he didn't look so darn appealing even trussed up like a rigid soldier.

'I'm sorry you've come all this way, but Gina's playing some warped trick on the both of us, sticking her nose where it isn't wanted when we both know you're duty bound to marry your perfect little chosen bride and live happily ever after.'

'But I love you,' he said, his steady, blue-eyed stare compelling, hypnotising.

Suddenly, the penny dropped. Not just one, but a whole bagful of screeching metal, crashing down on her conscious and making her see red.

'Let me guess, you want the dutiful wife at home and a Melbourne mistress on the side. Feed me a few pathetic lines of love, hope I'll wait around for you whenever you're in town, is that the general idea?'

She paused for a second, wishing the film of crimson mist in front of her eyes would clear so she could give him a proper staring down.

'Well, I've got news for you, Your Royal Delusional Highness. You can't just waltz back into my life and say you love me and think that makes everything okay. It just doesn't work that way. Besides, after what you've just implied, I wouldn't go near you if you were the last man on earth!'

So there.

Dante didn't move, he didn't flinch, but the blazing expression in his eyes made her want to take a step back.

'Maybe I can convince you otherwise?' he said, his voice soft, low, menacing.

'Forget it.'

She let her guard drop for a second, pleased with her unwavering front when inside she quaked like jelly, and before she knew it Dante had crossed the room, hauled her into his arms and locked his lips on hers.

'No—ooo...'

Her protest died on a moan as his lips gentled, coaxed, and finally triumphed when she opened her mouth beneath his, desperate for the first thrust of his tongue, meeting him, challenging him, wanting this kiss to last for ever.

Heat streaked through her body, waking her dormant libido with a jolt, making her want him with a desperate hunger.

She needed him. All of him.

Body to body, skin to skin, joined in an intimacy she'd never craved till this man had entered her life and turned her world upside down.

Her hands splayed against his chest, caught in the act of pushing him away, helpless to resist the pull of heat radiating from him. She basked in it, warming quickly, reaching burning point within seconds. Burning for him, only him, the only man she'd ever really loved.

*The man who is toying with you, again.*

She broke the kiss, annoyed, reluctant, breathless, her gaze drawn to his lips merely inches from hers.

'Tasha, look at me.'

He placed a finger under her chin and tilted her head up, gently, without force, giving her time to pull away if she wanted.

She didn't.

If she'd thought his body radiated heat, it had nothing on his eyes, the aquamarine depths a bubbling pool of molten blue heat, the hottest part of a flame, the most hypnotic, and the most seductive.

'I love you. Every stubborn, self-reliant, capable inch of you. You captured my heart from the first minute I saw you, and I didn't stand a chance. Maybe my approach needs some work but, forgive me, I have been trying to phrase my declaration exactly right. I want you to marry me, to trust in me enough to make a new beginning in a new country. This isn't a game or a ploy or some scenario playing out. This is about you and me, and the rest of our lives. If you want it to be.'

He wanted to *marry* her? Hope sparked deep in her soul, but her self-esteem had taken a beating once too often for her to jump up and down with joy just yet.

She'd heard smooth words before, practised words designed to deceive, to obtain an end goal.

She needed more.

She needed proof.

'If you love me, why did you leave? Why did you let me walk away when I'd laid my heart on the line?'

Dante didn't look away, his steady gaze unwavering and filled with a clear-eyed honesty which took her breath away.

'I was a fool. A man who's never been in love before doesn't know the symptoms, can't recognise the cure even when it's staring him in the face. I knew we were attracted to each other, I valued our friendship and I wanted more, but when I saw you with your ex something short-circuited in my brain.'

'You were jealous,' she said, trying to absorb the impact of his words without letting her topsy-turvy emotions get in the way.

'And stupid. In all honesty, I was probably looking for a way out, a way to explain away the feelings I didn't understand, and I took it. You made it easy to love you, but you also made it easy for me by giving me an excuse to walk away because I wanted to.'

He closed his eyes for a second, a pained expression crossing his face before opening them again.

'I didn't know what love was till I reached Calida. When I couldn't think, couldn't function, couldn't breathe without going mad for thinking about you.'

He cupped her cheeks, caressing her with his fingertips, sending shivers down her spine. 'Thinking about how beautiful you are, how your eyes spark golden when you're passionate about something.'

His thumbs brushed her lips, setting them tingling. 'How I only kissed you once in a bout of foolery, and how much I yearned to do it again. For the rest of my life.'

He kissed her, a soft, gentle melding of lips, a kiss of honesty, of hope. Her heart unfurled beneath it, filled with a burgeoning sense of infinite possibilities.

'Will you be my wife, Tasha? Be by my side, facing the future together?'

A vivid image of the two of them in bridal finery flashed before her eyes, a romantic picture to go with the romantic fairy-tale ending she'd never envisaged for herself.

Until now.

'I promise you everyone in Calida will come to love you as much as I do.'

Suddenly, her fantasy bubble popped, and reality set in with a vengeance.

She couldn't marry Dante, no matter how much she loved him.

They came from different worlds, a monstrous gulf of protocols and class and propriety separating them. She'd never been a snob, but she'd worked with his class of people her entire life, had seen the differences, the subtle ways which separated them from everyone else.

For some, like Dante, it wasn't a conscious thing, it was part of who he was, a birthright.

She would never fit in.

No matter how many etiquette lessons she had, no matter how hard she tried to blend in, she would never be good enough, and she'd had a gutful of having her self-esteem trampled, of feeling second best.

Dante loved her and that should've been enough.

But it wasn't. She'd heard about his mother, she'd seen the pushy, over-confident woman Gina was, and she couldn't stand up to that type of barrage long term. At the start, in the honeymoon period maybe, but sooner or later she'd find herself on the outside, and the thought of Dante's love turning to despair when he looked at his out-of-place wife made her want to run out the door that second and never look back.

'I'm sorry, I can't,' she said, stepping out of the comforting circle of his arms, cold loneliness replacing the warmth of his body.

His eyes widened with shock, his mouth a perfect O, as if he'd never dreamed she'd refuse him.

'Your answer is no?'

Natasha almost capitulated right then, hating

the pain slashing his proud features, knowing it must reflect her own.

She had no choice.

She had to make the logical decision, the safe decision, for the both of them.

'Dante, listen to me. You're an incredible man, but we're too different. We're worlds apart in every way, and I don't think I'm the right woman for you. Your bride, the future queen of your country, needs to be someone in sync with you, with your family, and unfortunately I don't fit the bill. I'm sorry.'

The words caught in her throat, her refusal every bit as painful as losing him had been. However, this time would be worse, so much worse, when he exited her life for now she knew he loved her.

Her heart turned over, warring with her head, urging her to throw every common sense reason why they shouldn't be together out the window and follow him to the ends of the earth if needed. But she'd never been the frivolous type, never would be. Life consisted of responsibilities, and she couldn't change how she thought, just like Dante couldn't change his birthright.

'I understand your concerns,' he said, not appearing fazed in the slightest at her refusal.

If anything, he'd squared his shoulders, stood taller, and the corners of his too-kissable mouth twitched as if he knew the punchline of some upcoming joke.

'You've made some valid points. Yes, we're different, and yes, our worlds are so far apart, but these obstacles can be overcome by one thing. And, as it happens, it's the one thing you haven't mentioned.'

'What's that?'

His eyes twinkled and he actually smiled, the familiar action setting her pulse racing double-time when it had barely slowed to an acceptable rate after that sizzling kiss.

'Love,' he said, pronouncing it with all the importance of bestowing a title on her. 'You've mentioned connections and the like, I've said I love you, but you haven't said you love me.'

'What makes you think I do?'

She avoided his gaze, looking anywhere but at those all-seeing eyes which wouldn't let her get away with anything let alone a blatant lie like that.

Silence descended, a taut, tension-fraught silence which stretched on for endless moments, the type of uncomfortable silence neither of them wished to break.

'If you say you don't love me, I'll leave. It's

as simple as that,' he said, his low voice compelling, urgent, tugging at her heartstrings, until she finally raised her eyes to his, knowing she couldn't do it.

She'd always been honest, brutally so at times, and now, when her future depended on a big, fat lie, she couldn't do it.

'Tasha?'

'I can't,' she said, shaking her head, knowing her answer would only complicate matters for both of them.

'You can't love me?'

For an impressive, macho guy, his tone wavered, and she captured his hands in hers, needing the physical contact to ground her, to get her through this.

'I can't lie to you,' she murmured, beseeching him to understand with her eyes, squeezing his hands for support. 'Of course I love you. Why do you think I came by your hotel that night? Why do you think I made a fool of myself there? I fell in love with you way too fast, and even now it scares me beyond belief. But love can't conquer all, Dante. Real life doesn't work like that. Being in love may get us through the early tough times, but you're a prince, soon to be king. Do you really think I'll be accepted into your world? Do you really think it isn't going to matter?'

She released one of his hands to reach up and caress his cheek, savouring the slight rasp of stubble against her palm. Though she appreciated his clean-shaven look, she liked the bad-boy unshaven look more.

'I'm a simple girl from Melbourne. I love my job, I love my friends, I love my family. It just wouldn't work out. As for Clay, I owed him money, money he once gave me for the hotel. What you saw was his pathetic attempt at asserting control over me, what you missed was me shoving him away.'

'You love me.'

He breathed the words on a breath of awe, sending a wave of pride over her that a guy like him loved a girl like her. 'Nothing else matters. Nothing. We can face the future, whatever it holds, together. You won't lose your friends or family. They can visit, and we'll spend more time in Melbourne.'

He pulled her close, locking his hands around her waist like he'd never let her go.

She wished.

'We can accomplish anything we want. Together. It has to be us together, always. I love you. I'll always love you.'

He rested his forehead on hers as if trying to transfer his thoughts by osmosis and she didn't move, content to be joined in some contact with the man she loved, the man she would always love.

*The man she would always love...*

There was her answer.

Rather simplistic, considering all the barriers she'd erected between them, all the perfectly legitimate excuses she'd made, but once the phrase lodged in her head she knew what she had to do.

Pulling away slightly, she slid her arms around his waist, enjoying their perfect fit.

'Dante?'

'Yes?'

She smiled. He never said 'yeah' like other guys, but a formal 'yes' that she could imagine him uttering to dignitaries across the world.

'You ever seen a movie called *The Princess Bride*?'

'No.'

Confusion warred with a tiny flicker of hope in his eyes, and she laughed, a purely happy sound for the first time in for ever.

'In that case, why don't we create our own version with me in the starring role?'

Realisation turned his eyes a startling blue and he let out a whoop of joy. 'Does that mean what I think it means?'

'It means you're about to be stuck with me for better or worse.'

He picked her up and swung her around, till they both staggered in a dizzy embrace.

She slid down his body, joy bubbling within her, spreading its incredible heat through her body like warm treacle. Or that could've been the obvious evidence of just how happy her future husband was with her declaration.

'We're going to live happily ever after in a big castle. You know that, don't you?'

Natasha smiled and traced her fiancé's lips with her fingertip. 'I know that I love you. I know that you're a wonderful guy. And I know that I finally believe in fairy tales.'

'So how does *The Princess Bride* end?' he whispered, kissing his way from her hand to her arm and slowly upwards, his lips trailing across her neck to the soft skin beneath her ear as she gasped in delight.

'Stick with me and you'll find out,' she said, smiling as his lips finally settled over hers, and she lost herself in the magic of his kiss, looking forward to creating a happy ending all of their own.

\* \* \* \* \*

# THE ROYAL HOUSE OF NIROLI
*Always passionate, always proud*

The richest royal family in the world—
united by blood and passion,
torn apart by deceit and desire

Nestled in the azure blue of the Mediterranean Sea, the majestic island of Niroli has prospered for centuries. The Fierezza men have worn the crown with passion and pride since ancient times. But now, as the king's health declines, and his two sons have been tragically killed, the crown is in jeopardy.

The clock is ticking—a new heir must be found before the king is forced to abdicate. By royal decree the internationally scattered members of the Fierezza family are summoned to claim their destiny. But any person who takes the throne must do so according to The Rules of the Royal House of Niroli. Soon secrets and rivalries emerge as the descendents of this ancient royal line vie for position and power. Only a true Fierezza can become ruler—a person dedicated to their country, their people...and their eternal love!

*Each month starting in July 2007,*
*Harlequin Presents is delighted to bring you*
*an exciting installment from*
THE ROYAL HOUSE OF NIROLI,
*in which you can follow the epic search*
*for the true Nirolian king.*
*Eight heirs, eight romances, eight fantastic stories!*

Here's your chance to enjoy a sneak preview of the first book delivered to you by royal decree...

FIVE minutes later she was standing immobile in front of the study's window, her original purpose of coming in forgotten, as she stared in shocked horror at the envelope she was holding. Waves of heat followed by icy chill surged through her body. She could hardly see the address now through her blurred vision, but the crest on its left-hand front corner stood out, its *royal* crest, followed by the address: *HRH Prince Marco of Niroli...*

She didn't hear Marco's key in the apartment door, she didn't even hear him calling out her name. Her shock was so great that nothing could penetrate it. It encased her in a kind of bubble, which only concentrated the torment of what she was suffering and branded it on her brain so that it could never be forgotten. It was only finally pierced by the sudden opening of the study door as Marco walked in.

"Welcome home, *Your Highness*. I suppose I ought to curtsy." She waited, praying that he would laugh and tell her that she had got it all wrong, that the envelope she was holding, addressing him as Prince Marco of Niroli, was some silly mistake. But like a tiny candle flame shivering vulnerably in the dark, her hope trembled fearfully. And then the look in Marco's eyes extinguished it as cruelly as a hand placed callously over a dying person's face to stem their last breath.

"Give that to me," he demanded, taking the envelope from her.

"It's too late, Marco," Emily told him brokenly. "I know the truth now…." She dug her teeth in her lower lip to try to force back her own pain.

"You had no right to go through my desk," Marco shot back at her furiously, full of loathing at being caught off-guard and forced into a position in which he was in the wrong, making him determined to find something he could accuse Emily of. "I trusted you…."

Emily could hardly believe what she was hearing. "No, you didn't trust me, Marco, and you didn't trust me because you knew that I couldn't trust you. And you knew that because you're a liar, and liars don't trust people because they know that they themselves cannot be trusted." She not only felt sick, she also felt as though she could hardly breathe. "You are Prince Marco of Niroli.... How could you not tell me who you are and still live with me as intimately as we have lived together?" she demanded brokenly.

"Stop being so ridiculously dramatic," Marco demanded fiercely. "You are making too much of the situation."

"*Too much?*" Emily almost screamed the words at him. "When were you going to tell me, Marco? Perhaps you just planned to walk away without telling me anything? After all, what do my feelings matter to you?"

"Of course they matter." Marco stopped her sharply. "And it was in part to protect them, and you, that I decided not to inform you when my grandfather first announced that he intended to step down from the throne and hand it on to me."

"To protect me?" Emily nearly choked on her fury. "Hand on the throne? No wonder you told me when you first took me to bed that all you wanted was sex. You *knew* that was the only kind of relationship there could ever be between us! You *knew* that one day you would be Niroli's king. No doubt you are expected to marry a princess. Is she picked out for you already, your *royal* bride?"

\* \* \* \* \*

*Look for*
*THE FUTURE KING'S PREGNANT MISTRESS*
*by Penny Jordan in July 2007,*
*from Harlequin Presents,*
*available wherever books are sold.*

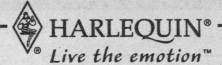

# HARLEQUIN®
## *Live the emotion*™

The series you love are now available in

# LARGER PRINT!

The books are complete and unabridged—
printed in a larger type size to make it
easier on your eyes.

**HARLEQUIN®**

**HARLEQUIN ROMANCE®**

*From the Heart, For the Heart*

**HARLEQUIN®**

# INTRIGUE

*Breathtaking Romantic Suspense*

**HARLEQUIN®**
*Presents*

Seduction and Passion Guaranteed!

**HARLEQUIN®**
*Super Romance*®

*Exciting, Emotional, Unexpected*

## Try LARGER PRINT today!
Visit: www.eHarlequin.com
Call: 1-800-873-8635

HLPDIR07

HARLEQUIN®

 ROMANCE®

# Invites *you* to experience lively, heartwarming all-American romances

Every month, we bring you four strong, sexy men, and four women who know what they want—and go all out to get it.

From small towns to big cities, experience a sense of adventure, romance and family spirit—the all-American way!

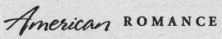 ROMANCE

## Heart, Home & Happiness

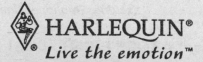 HARLEQUIN®
*Live the emotion*™

www.eHarlequin.com                    HARDIR06

# HARLEQUIN®
# INTRIGUE®

## BREATHTAKING ROMANTIC SUSPENSE

Shared dangers and passions lead to electrifying romance and heart-stopping suspense!

Every month, you'll meet six new heroes who are guaranteed to make your spine tingle and your pulse pound. With them you'll enter into the exciting world of Harlequin Intrigue— where your life is on the line and so is your heart!

## THAT'S INTRIGUE— ROMANTIC SUSPENSE AT ITS BEST!

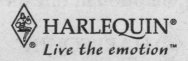

HARLEQUIN®
*Live the emotion*™

**www.eHarlequin.com**            INTDIR06

# HARLEQUIN®

## *SuperRomance*®

# ...there's more to the story!

**Superromance.**
A *big* satisfying read about unforgettable
characters. Each month we offer *six* very different
stories that range from family drama to adventure
and mystery, from highly emotional stories to
romantic comedies—and much more! Stories
about people you'll believe in and care about.
Stories too compelling to put down....

Our authors are among today's *best* romance
writers. You'll find familiar names and talented
newcomers. Many of them are award winners—
and you'll see why!

If you want the biggest and best
in romance fiction, you'll get it
from Superromance!

## Exciting, Emotional, Unexpected...

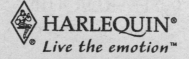

### HARLEQUIN®
*Live the emotion*™

www.eHarlequin.com

HSDIR06

## Harlequin® Historical
### Historical Romantic Adventure!

*Imagine a time of chivalrous
knights and unconventional ladies,
roguish rakes and impetuous
heiresses, rugged cowboys
and spirited frontierswomen—
these rich and vivid tales will
capture your imagination!*

*Harlequin Historical . . .
they're too good to miss!*

**www.eHarlequin.com**     HHDIR06

## V Silhouette®

# SPECIAL EDITION™

## Emotional, compelling stories that capture the intensity of living, loving and creating a family in today's world.

Special Edition features bestselling authors such as Susan Mallery, Sherryl Woods, Christine Rimmer, Joan Elliott Pickart— and many more!

For a romantic, complex and emotional read, choose Silhouette Special Edition.

## V Silhouette®

Visit Silhouette Books at www.eHarlequin.com

SSEGEN06